I0667858

JINGLED AND JANGLED

A DELIGHTFULLY DYSFUNCTIONAL FAMILIAL CHRISTMAS

THE DELIGHTFULLY DYSFUNCTIONAL SERIES
BOOK #2

A NOVEL

TIFFANY RYAN

Copyright 2023 Tiffany Ryan

All rights reserved.

No part of this book may be reproduced in any form without the written permission from the author, other than for the use of brief quotations in the book.

This book is a work of fiction. Names, characters, places, and incidents are purely the product of the author's imagination and are used fictitiously. Any similarities to actual events, locales, or persons, living or dead, is completely coincidental.

Paperback ISBN: 979-8-9886983-2-6
Ebook ISBN: 979-8-9886983-3-3

This book is dedicated to my mother, Kathi.

I love you.

Chapter One

"I can't believe you're drinking wine while making me suffer through all this extra homework," said Beau irritably. "No one else's mom ever makes them do this."

"I can't believe you received such a poor grade on something you knew how to do," my mother replied casually, "And I'm not everyone else's mom, I'm your mom."

"I can't believe you won't just let this go," he grumbled.

"I can't believe you think that I would," she countered.

"I can't believe you're making me re-work everything!"

She poured more wine into her glass, "I can't believe you think that I wouldn't."

"Ugh, I can't believe this!" he wailed.

She lifted her glass in mock salutation, "I can, hence the wine."

Once Beau's tirade was over, he quietly finished the last few problems on the page and then handed it over to my mother for inspection, "Would you like a vial of my blood too?"

Mom carefully studied over the page, and after seeing that it was error free, took her red felt-tip pen, wrote a number in the top right-hand corner, and handed it back to him, "No need for blood, your torment and despair over the past hour were reward enough for me." She then smiled warmly and let her tone soften a bit, "Listen, I know you may think of me as harsh sometimes, but I love you more than anything else in this world. There isn't anything I wouldn't do for you, and that includes making sure that you understand that certain behaviors illicit certain consequences. I know it isn't a fun lesson, but it's one that you need to learn in order to make your way in this world." She cupped his cheek lovingly, "I don't like having to be the bad guy, Beau, I really don't, but I would be doing you a disservice if I didn't at least try to teach you right from wrong. Please tell me you understand what I'm saying."

"Yeah, I do," he smiled, "and don't worry, mom, I know you love me."

"Okay, good." She wiped away an errant tear and kissed him on the cheek, "Why don't you go on up and play your Xbox for a bit, and I'll call you down when dinner's ready."

"Yes, ma'am." He stood to leave and then immediately sat back down, "An 85?" he asked incredulously. "But I got them all correct!"

"Not initially, you didn't," she said. "That alone lost you 10 points right there."

"Which leaves me with a 90, but you gave me an 85," he said pointing at the bright red number on the page.

"Oh, you caught that did you?" she grinned mischievously and winked, "Yes, well, your snarky little comment about the blood knocked off an additional five."

"Wait, what?" he shook his head in disbelief. "You can't do that!"

"Yes, I can, I'm the teacher." Mom stood up from the table and crossed her arms in front of her, "You would do well to let this serve as a lesson to you, Beau, that taking the easy way out is not only feckless, but indolent," she then added, "That means irresponsible and lazy, by the way."

"Oh, great, another life lesson I didn't ask for," he said glumly. He picked up his books and slowly tromped up the stairs, "I hate my life, I hate my life, I hate my life."

"And that's why God put me on this earth, honey, to make your life miserable," she smiled sweetly, "You just let me know if there's anything else I can do to make your stay here even worse."

"Well, so far, it's been a five-star experience, so I'd say you've done your job," he retorted sourly.

This is the daily back and forth discourse that often takes place between my mother and her youngest male progeny, who despite being incredibly smart, is always looking for the easiest and quickest way out of situations, especially when it comes to school. You see, my brother and I are both homeschooled, which means while other kids are at school enjoying a break from their family, we are at home enduring a constant state of learning and togetherness that, truth be told, often takes a toll on my mother's mental well-being, which is the main reason you will frequently find her sipping chardonnay and integrating words like feckless and indolent into everyday conversation. My older brother, Ezra, graduated last year, and I will this coming May, but Beau still has another four years, which if I'm being completely honest, is probably what drives her to drink. As for me, my name is Adelaide Jenkins, middle child, proud member, and self-proclaimed chronicler of said fanatical family.

"Little pissant," she mumbled under her breath. "That child is beyond smart but refuses to put in the effort. What does he expect, milk and cookies?" She started clearing off the table and turned her attention over to me, "Addie, honey, how much more reading do you have left?"

I was so engrossed in the story that I never even heard her call my name.

"Addie, did you hear me?" she asked.

"What's that?" I said looking up from my book.

"I was asking how much more reading you had," she said.

"Oh, I'm just about done." I referenced the book I was holding, "This is so good!"

"Oh, my gosh, I know!" She scampered excitedly over to me and took a seat. "I was thinking that you may want to write about the different cultural aspects between the two main characters and then highlight how it's those very aspects that wind up driving them apart in the end. Not only would that enable you to shed some anthropological insight into your paper, but also showcase your ability to internalize the social and cultural constructs that affected many indigenous societies at that time." She took a breath, "What do you think?"

"Honestly? I think you're trying to live out your anthropological fantasies vicariously through me and my writing," I said.

Over the years, my mother has tried ceaselessly to get at least one of her children interested in the study of anthropology, but to no avail. Her own dream of becoming a renowned anthropologist was cut short the minute Grandma Helen realized that there was very little money to be made without a PhD and institutional backing. Knowing full well that mom's collegiate future was determined by the very hand that fed her, she chose to major in a much more practical discipline, namely accounting. And although it galled Grandma Helen to no end that her youngest daughter chose to minor in anthropology, a subject she believed was dedicated to, and I quote, "Digging in the dirt, flint knapping, and archaic cultures with clicking tongues," she and mom were eventually able to make peace despite the fact Grandma Helen still refuses to recognize the study as anything other than "the glorified trash picking of dead people."

"Fine, be that way," said mom. She sullenly walked back into the kitchen to retrieve her wine glass, "But just so you know, I would have killed to write a paper like that when I was your age."

"And what kind of paper would that be, dear?" asked Grandma Helen strolling casually through the back door.

"Oh, you know, just an insightful anthropological look into the differing cultural aspects that are currently presenting themselves in the book Addie is reading."

"Ugh, anthropology," she shuddered. "Every time I hear you utter that word it makes me feel dirty and in need of a hot shower." She picked up an envelope sitting on the counter and studied it, "Honestly, Olivia, I've never quite understood your fascination and desire to sift through dirt in search of the decaying remnants of dead people." She looked back up at mom, "It's really quite morbid and sad."

"Are you finished?" asked mom plucking the envelope out of Grandma Helen's hand, "And that's archaeology, mother, which is only one facet of anthropology, and in no way represents the entire scope of the profession."

"Archaeology, anthropology, African Anteater Dance," she shrugged, "It's all dull and boring to me, dear." She breathed in deeply and spread her arms out in a theatrical display, "Now, give me a stage, an adoring audience, and a good script to work with, and you will find me rapt with attention."

A few years ago, Grandma Helen decided to join the local community theater group in the hopes of better adjusting to retirement after she and Grandpa Anthony sold their two highly successful Italian restaurants. That was on a Tuesday; by Thursday she had quickly come to the realization that seclusion and anonymity were most certainly not her friends, and immediately sought out a way to find the excitement and attention she craved. When the restaurants were open, she was the consummate star and socialite that everyone clamored around, while Grandpa Anthony was the man behind the scenes, whipping up award winning Italian food to satiate her adoring public. Once she realized that part of her life was over, she went in search of something that would give her the same kind of thrill, so she decided to audition for a small part in the local production of *My Fair Lady,* and after winning the lead role as Eliza Doolittle, she was completely hooked. Since then, she has been cast as a lead in every production and is currently petitioning the theater's board of directors to allow her take on the starring role of Eve Ensler in *The Vagina Monologues,* a feat that is proving to be slightly more difficult than she had first anticipated.

"Yes, well, we didn't ask for your opinion, mother." Mom pointed to her wine glass, "Would you like a glass of wine?"

"Is the Pope Catholic?" she asked.

"Last time I checked, yes." Mom pulled the wine from the refrigerator and filled both of their glasses, "So, any news on your bid for *The Vagina Monologues?*"

"I don't think it's going to happen," she sighed. "Honestly, those people wouldn't know good theater if it turned around and bit them in the ass." She sipped her wine, "Apparently, the idea of a story based on the female vagina is considered too much for small town Georgia."

"They turned you down, Grandma?" I said coming into the kitchen.

"Unfortunately, dear, yes." She stared solemnly into her glass, "They seem to think that some of the topics may trigger people and make them feel uncomfortable."

"Well, to be fair, it does delve into some fairly serious issues," said mom.

"What do you mean?" I asked. "What Issues?"

"Well, I'm certainly no authority on the topic, but if I recall correctly, the play focuses primarily on the everyday aspects of the feminine experience, both good and bad." Mom took some ground beef out of the refrigerator and set it on the counter, "So, while there are some funny discussions about love and sex, there are also some not so funny discussions about rape and genital mutilation."

"Oh, my gosh, that actually happens?" I gasped. "Why would anyone ever do something like that to someone?"

"It actually happens a lot more often than you think, especially in male dominated societies," said mom.

"Huh, and here I thought it was just a humorous foray into the life of one woman and her vagina," shrugged Grandma Helen, "I guess you learn something new every day."

"Wait, didn't you at least do a little bit of research prior to submitting your request to the board?" asked mom.

"Well, I watched a few short videos on YouTube, if that's what you mean," she answered plainly.

"So, you're telling me that you haven't even watched the play in its entirety?" Mom raised her hands in mock surrender, "You know what, never mind, I think the board is right; it's probably too risqué for this town, anyway." She pulled a pan out from under the cabinet and began browning the meat, "Honestly, mother, I can't believe you never even watched the play that you were so adamant about producing and starring in."

"I don't know why you're getting so upset, Olivia, it's not like you were the one wanting the part. Besides," she waved her hand dismissively "I now have bigger and better things on the horizon."

"Oh, and what might those be?" asked mom skeptically raising her brow.

"Well, it's still in the infant stages of planning, but you are currently looking at the future star of one of the greatest musicals ever made." She smiled coyly and then began clapping her hands excitedly, "I'm going to be playing Sandra Dee in the musical *Grease!*"

Mom reflexively choked on her wine, barely keeping it from spewing out, "I'm sorry, did you just say *Grease?* The film about Pink Ladies, T-Birds, and rowdy teenagers living in 1950's America?"

"Can you believe it?" beamed Grandma Helen. "This role was made for me!"

Mom cleared her throat delicately, "Don't you think you might be a little too-"

"Careful, Olivia," Grandma Helen sang sweetly, "You don't want to say something you may come to regret later."

"Okay, let me rephrase it, then." She cleared her throat again, "Don't you think it may be a bit out of your wheelhouse, being the venerable thespian that you are, to take on a role that will require you to portray a giddy lovesick teenage schoolgirl prancing around in a poodle skirt? I mean, you're 74 years old, don't you think you might just be a wee bit past your prime on this one?"

"That was both ageist and insulting, dear," glared Grandma Helen.

"Look, mom, I'm not trying to offend you," said mom penitently, "I'm just trying to get you to see reason." She seasoned the meat in the pan, "I've always been supportive, so please know that I'm only hesitant because I don't want to see you made a fool of."

"I'm not going to be made a fool of, darling," she said dismissively. "Besides, *Grease* is one of the most popular musicals in the history of musicals, so what better way to showcase my skill as an actor than to take on the one role that will challenge me most?" She took another sip of wine and sneered, "Not to mention the fact that me stepping away will only encourage Joan to snatch up the part, and if you think I'm going to let her do that, well…" she laughed bitterly, "You are sadly mistaken."

Joan Humphries, formerly known as Satan's Mistress, is Grandma Helen's biggest rival and most significant challenger to any-and-all starring roles in the theater. I say formerly because the two, who were at one time bitter enemies (at least as far as Grandma Helen was concerned), are now relatively good friends who often find themselves shopping, rehearsing, and dining together quite regularly. This transition from arch nemeses to frenemies took place around seven months ago during Grandma Helen's birthday celebration when Joan made a surprise appearance at Sullivan's Cocktail Lounge for amateur karaoke night. The animosity oozing out of Grandma Helen was palpable that night, and it wasn't until Joan graciously and unselfishly conceded her bid for a role and openly admitted her admiration for Grandma Helen, that everything turned around, and a friendship, albeit an unconventional one, came to fruition.

"I thought you and Joan were friends, Grandma," I said confusedly.

"We are, dear, but that doesn't mean I want to see her succeed at my expense," she snickered. "Besides, Joan often struggles with the higher notes, so I wouldn't be much of a friend if I allowed her to debase herself in front of an audience trying to hit one."

"Once again, mother, your ability to put other's needs in front of your own is simply astounding." Mom carefully stirred the meat in the pan and then added, "I'm curious though, who did they decide to cast as Danny Zuko?"

"I believe that part went to Walter," said Grandma Helen. "He's by far the best baritone we have, so it seems fitting."

"Walter? Mom, he just had a hip replacement two months ago. How in the world is he planning to gyrate across the stage singing to Greased Lightnin'?"

"I haven't a clue dear," she finished her wine, "But I'm sure we'll cross that bridge when we inevitably come to it." She stood and peered over the counter to see what mom was cooking, "What is that, anyway?"

"Taco meat," said mom grating some cheese, "Would you and dad like to join us for dinner? We have plenty."

"Yeah, stay for dinner, Grandma." I said grabbing some plates out of the cabinet, "I'd be happy to set two more place settings."

"Thank you, dear, but your grandfather is out with some friends playing trivia and, well, as much as I love good Mexican food," she scrunched up her nose, "Your mothers doesn't really fall into that category." She smiled brightly, walked over to the back door, and blew us both a kiss, "Well, I'm off to enjoy a Lean Cuisine, ta ta, my darlings!"

CHAPTER TWO

Later that night, mom was relaxing on the couch watching *Skate America*, one of six ISU Grand Prix Figure Skating Championships that take place in various countries around the world. These yearly events, which typically fill the entire months of October, November, and December, are the precursor to the crème de la crème of all things figure skating, the World Championships, unless it's an Olympic year, which of course would then take precedence. Now, you may be wondering how a soccer player, such as myself, has come to know so much about the sport of figure skating, well, the simplest answer to that question, would be my mother. You see, mom was once a figure skater herself long ago, and even though no one in our family has ever seen her skate, she insists that she was once very competitive. We have tried to get her to go skating multiple times, but since she can no longer fit into her old skates and would rather die than lace up a pair of rentals, we have no choice but to take her word for it. My dad and brothers do their best to avoid the living room at all costs whenever skating is on, but sometimes, like tonight, one of them gets caught unaware and winds up succumbing to my mother's endless tirade about cheated jumps, traveling spins, and the ever popular, "I can't believe they took figures out of figure skating" soliloquy.

"Oh, lovely, it's that time again, is it?" said Ezra. He came downstairs and walked into the kitchen, "Every time I think we're in the clear, it comes back with a vengeance."

"You know, your father gives me enough crap about watching ice skating, Ezra, I don't need you adding your two cents," she said.

"But what I have to say is always so enlightening, mother." He pulled some turkey and cheese from the refrigerator and immediately stopped, dumbfounded by what he saw staring back at him on the TV screen, "Ew, what is that?"

"Oh, that's Johnny Weir," she said turning down the volume. "He and Tara are always the commentators for nationally televised skating events."

"Tara?" he asked.

"Lipinski." Taking note of Ezra's vacuous stare, she sighed heavily, "She's an Olympic gold medalist?"

"Never heard of her." He grabbed some bread from the pantry, "And why exactly is that guy's hair coiffed two feet off his head? If I didn't know any better, I'd think he was a tribute representing the first district in the *Hunger Games*."

"He's slightly over the top, Ezra, yes, but he's good at what he does." She turned her attention back to the TV, "And he was a truly beautiful skater, so a little respect is in order."

"Oh, it's Johnny!" squealed Grandma Helen in delight "I just adore him." She came in through the back door and sat down excitedly across from mom, "I know he can be a bit eccentric, but I always find myself agreeing with everything he has to say." She propped her feet up on the ottoman, "And he and Tara always look so cute together."

"If you say so," said Ezra unassumingly making a sandwich.

"Okay, shh, everyone," said mom. "I really want to see this next skater."

"And who is this, dear?" asked Grandma Helen.

"I can't remember his name, but he can do a quad axel!" said mom. "He's the first person to ever land one in competition."

"Well, quadruple axel or not, that outfit is simply horrid," sneered Grandma Helen. "The least he could do is spruce it up a bit and make someone actually want to watch him careen around the ice for four minutes."

"Noted, mother," nodded mom.

"And that music is absolutely atrocious," she shuddered. "It sounds like the muffled cries of a baby goat."

Mom paused the television and irritably stared her down, "Do you mind?"

"Not at all, dear," she waved her hand dismissively and walked over to Ezra, "Your mother is always so uptight whenever she watches skating." She helped herself to one of his chips, "Honestly, you would think she was Sonja Henie incarnate the way she carries on." She sidled up next to him and spoke in a fake stage whisper "The child could barely land a single axel and yet she now fancies herself as some sort of figure skating guru."

"Why are you still talking, mother?" she turned off the TV and joined the two of them in the kitchen, "And just for the record, that single axel is what allowed me to win all of those competitions back in the day."

"Yes, that preliminary girl's division was just viscous, dear, wasn't it?" she drawled.

"Look. I don't even know what you two are talking about, but I think I've had enough skating for tonight," said Ezra. "I think I'll go watch *Full Metal Jacket* and redeem my masculinity." As he turned to make his way upstairs, mom called out after him, "Oh, and just so you know, we'll be trimming the tree as a family Friday night, and I fully expect you to be a willing and compliant participant."

"I can't, I have plans with Sabrina that night," he said.

"Bring her with you," said mom. "I'd love to have the opportunity get to know her a little bit better." She lowered her voice, "Lord knows you sure have."

A few months ago, mom caught Ezra slinking home after an evening tryst with his girlfriend, Sabrina, and once she finally got over the shock and utter despair of knowing that her innocent baby boy was no longer innocent, she has worked tirelessly to convince him to bring her around so that the family can interrogate…I mean, become better acquainted with her.

"I'm not sure I'm ready for that kind of commitment, besides," he gestured toward the TV, "we wouldn't want to impose on your little skating party with Tara and Johnny."

"Nice try, but the joke is on you, my friend," she snarked. "It's only ice dancing and since Tara and Johnny are not experts in that genre of skating, they won't be on air that day."

"You know, I rather prefer the ice dancing, myself," interjected Grandma Helen. "The costumes are always so much more interesting and usually follow along with a theme, which makes it far more engaging for the observer. In fact, there's this one couple that do a magnificent job of portraying an astronaut and alien…"

"Not now, mother," interrupted mom.

Turning back toward Ezra she said, "First of all, the sarcasm needs to go. I endured entirely too many hours of *The Wiggles*, *Teletubbies*, and that god awful *Caillou* character when you were a child to have you stand here and give me crap about watching ice skating."

"Oh, God that was awful," said Grandma Helen. "I was beyond grateful the day you grew out of that, dear."

"Secondly," continued mom, "You have been deliberately ignoring and avoiding any-and-all requests I've made for you to bring Sabrina here, so I'm simply going to put my foot down and tell you to do it. Your father and I would both like to meet this girl. She's obviously important to you, so it's not surprising that it would be important for us to get to know her." She let her tone soften a bit, "It's been months, Ezra, it's time to bring her here to meet your family."

He stared down at his feet for a few seconds before finally relenting, "Ugh, fine, I'll see if she's up for a rollicking night of tree trimming and Jenkin's merriment when I talk to her later tonight."

She lovingly touched his face and kissed his cheek, "I promise I won't embarrass you too much."

"Unfortunately, dear, I can't second that promise, but I can ensure that there will be plenty of alcohol to make it more bearable," said Grandma Helen.

"He's only 20, mother," said mom.

Oh, well, then, I guess that means it will be more bearable for us than it will be for you, but I'm sure you'll come through just fine, dear, you've always been a fighter."

"Okay, I'm not even sure what any of that means, but thanks, grandma." He ran up the stairs and called out, "And don't worry about us we'll just chug a few Colt 45's before heading this way."

"He used to be such a cordial child," mused Grandma Helen, "Now he's just sour and sardonic." She took a deep breath, "Oh well, I suppose it comes with the territory." She followed mom into the kitchen, "So, do you know anything about this girl?"

"Not really," said mom. "Ever since I caught him with that giant hickey on his neck, he's been incredibly tight-lipped about both she and their relationship." She picked up a bottle of pinot noir sitting on the counter and pulled two glasses from the wine cabinet, "I just pray he's making smart decisions, that's all."

"Well, you've always been very communicative with your children, darling, so I'm sure he hears your nagging little voice in the back of his head every time he takes his pants off." Grandma Helen gratefully accepted the glass of wine being offered, "And, if it makes you feel any better, you can always wrap up a box of condoms and present them as a little 'welcome to the family' gift." She winked over at mom, "I'm sure Ezra and Sabrina would be thrilled to know that you're taking an active interest in their love life."

"Have you completely lost your mind? Ezra would kill me if I did something like that!" She opened the refrigerator and pulled out some cheese, prosciutto, and salami, and then stopped dead in her tracks glaring directly over at Grandma Helen, "And don't you even think about it, mother, I will never forgive you if you make us look even more unorthodox than we already are."

"Now, why would I ever do something like that, darling?" she asked innocently.

"Because you thrive on being idiosyncratic and sharing your lunacy with others," said mom. "Sabrina will have enough to contend with, she doesn't need you swooping in and making her feel even more uncomfortable than she inevitably already will." She plated the cheese and meat along with some crackers, "That poor girl will probably be running for the hills after an hour with our family anyway, so I highly doubt she'll be needing the extra shove that might come from a box of beautifully wrapped contraceptives."

"Party pooper," sulked Grandma Helen. She took a sip of wine and immediately released it back into her glass. "Oh, dear God, what is this disgusting swill?"

"I don't know," said mom scrutinizing the bottle. "Some low-calorie wine Christine brought home the other night." She took a tentative sip and involuntarily shuddered, "Oh, God, that really is bad."

Grandma Helen immediately poured the contents of her glass down the drain, "If I didn't need the extra security of a second place to live, I would seriously disown that child purely on the basis of her poor palate." She picked up the bottle, "This is nothing more than grape mutilation, Olivia."

"Hey, I'm not the one that darkened our door with that stuff," said mom grabbing a different bottle from the wine cabinet. "Here, this should be better, Greg brought it home from Napa Valley when he was there a few months ago."

"Where is your husband, anyway?" asked Grandma Helen.

Mom opened the new bottle and poured them each a glass, "He's traveling for work, but should be back on Thursday."

As the two of them discussed dad's current trip to New Orleans, I walked through the back door holding a bouquet of wildflowers with a huge grin on my face.

"Well, how was it?" asked mom excitedly.

"How was what?" asked Grandma Helen.

"I had a date, grandma," I said kissing her on the cheek, "And it was amazing!"

"A date?" Her voice went up an octave before looking accusingly over at mom, "And why pray tell did you neglect to tell me that our darling little Adelaide was out with a gentleman caller?"

"Mom, we're no longer living in the 1940's, so please stop referencing men as gentleman callers." Mom draped her arm around my shoulder, "And I didn't tell you because you have a tendency to be overly judgmental at times, and are rarely, if ever, kind about it, so in order to avoid said judgment, we figured it would be best to just keep it on the downlow for a while."

"The downlow?" she reiterated snidely, "You're not a thug, Olivia, so please refrain from using slang words one would hear living in the slums of Los Angeles." She lowered her voice conspiratorially and then said, "Now, tell me all about this date!"

CHAPTER THREE

"Well," I drawled out slowly, but Grandma Helen in her haste to get to the point, immediately cut me off and went into interrogation mode.

"What's his name? Is he tall? Well-mannered? Educated? Is he a gentleman? Does he open your doors?" She lovingly reached for my hand, "More importantly, dear, does his family come from money or own a local winery, perhaps?"

"Take a breath, mom, geez! You're not even giving her any time to answer your questions." Mom looked pointedly over at me and arched her brow, "Do they own a winery?"

"I don't believe so, no," I laughed, "but, to answer your other questions, yes, he is taller than me, yes, he was both well-mannered and gentlemanly, and yes, he opened all of my doors." I lifted the bouquet, "And he brought me these beautiful flowers."

"Yes, I noticed those when you walked in," said Grandma Helen snidely, "tell me, did he gather them off the side of the road or buy them at Walmart?"

"Mother, don't be rude!" Mom turned to me and smiled warmly, "It was very kind of him to bring those to you, Addie, they're lovely."

"They look as if they were grown outside of a barn," mumbled Grandma Helen.

Taking immediate notice of mom's death stare, she quickly switched gears, "And what exactly is this boy's name, dear?"

"Dusty Dixon." I smiled.

"Dusty?" she curled her lip.

"Yes, grandma," I said.

She slowly enunciated it again, breaking the name up by its syllables, "Dusty?"

I nodded my head in agreement.

She sipped her wine contemplatively and then asked, "You mean like the fluffy gray substance constantly permeating your mother's furniture, dusty?"

"Yes, mother, Dusty," said mom irritably.

"There's no need to snap, Olivia, I'm simply seeking clarification." She turned her attention back over to me, "So, tell me, dear, what's he like?"

"Well, he's 17, loves to fish and hunt, works part time with his dad, who is an electrician, and loves to work on cars." I grabbed a vase and began filling it with water, "He's a true country boy and also one of the funniest people I know."

"Now, when you say country," drawled Grandma Helen slowly, "are we talking banjo playing I don't have my teeth, country, or something more along the lines of a Nashville, I look like a normal person, country?"

"Stop judging, mother, he's a lovely boy," said mom.

"I'm simply trying to get a better idea of what we're dealing with, here, darling." She lovingly stroked my hair, "I don't know about you, Olivia, but I for one, have no desire to see my beautiful granddaughter riding around town in an old beat-up Chevy pickup truck with a Confederate Flag waving off the back." She delicately placed a loose strand of hair behind my ear and whispered, "He doesn't have one of those now does he, dear?"

"Yes, mother, he proudly drives around town with a giant rebel flag painted on the roof of his vehicle, just like the General Lee in the *Dukes of Hazzard*," said mom. "In fact, Addie and I were just discussing the other day about how we needed to buy her some Daisy Dukes so that she could really authenticate the look while riding by his side on the bench seat of his 1975 Ford pickup."

"I'm glad you find all of this so amusing, dear," smirked Grandma Helen. "You know, it's because of you and your sister's disastrous foray into the dating world that I even worry." She shook her head solemnly, "The two of you would always bring home such peculiar and anomalous suitors, and try as hard as we might, your father and I could never quite understand what it was that attracted you to some of these boys."

"This sounds interesting," I said taking a seat next to Grandma Helen.

"It's really not," dismissed mom, "it was a long time ago, and I have since moved on." She added meat to the charcuterie board, "In fact, I think we all should."

Completely ignoring mom's suggestion, Grandma Helen continued, "Do you remember that boy you dated who was so obsessed with the *Karate Kid* and always wore that silly little headband with the Japanese symbol on it?"

"Not really, no," said mom.

"Surely you do, dear." She reached for a cracker and placed a slice of gouda and salami on top, "He always used to make us add 'San' to the end of his name and insisted on wearing that karate Gi everywhere he went, remember?"

"Oh, this is rich," I laughed. "So, what was his name?"

Mom mumbled incoherently while shoving a cracker into her mouth.

"I'm sorry, what was that dear?" snarked Grandma Helen.

She choked down the cracker and rolled her eyes, "Trevor-San, and I only went out with him because he looked exactly like Johnny Lawrence from that same movie."

"And then there was the boy I caught chugging Kaopectate in the bathroom that one time," snickered Grandma Helen. "He literally drank every last drop out of that bottle, and when I asked if his stomach was upset, he simply shook his head and said that he just really liked the taste of it." She sighed audibly, "Of course, then I had to remember to hide it from him any time he came over to the house, which if I'm being honest, was a daunting task in and of itself."

"Okay, that was Christine, not me," said mom.

"Oh, I know," Grandma Helen snapped her fingers excitedly, "weren't you the one who went out with that boy who constantly made all the different bird calls and then made you guess which ones they were?"

"Yes, that was Lark," said mom.

"Lark, as in the bird?" I asked incredulously.

"Unfortunately, yes," she rolled her eyes. "Lark always felt that his name somehow made him one with the birds, and since he fancied himself to be a bit of a bird whisperer, he always wanted to communicate with them, unsuccessfully I might add." She laughed inwardly, "I remember this one time he got too close to a blue jay nest and had upset them so much that they began charging after him, swooping and diving down as he screamed, and then as he ran away, I could hear him alternating between screams and bird calls in order to get them to stop, but they just kept chasing him. Poor Lark's whistling protests must have somehow gotten lost in translation because they just kept getting angrier and angrier."

The three of us were laughing so hysterically at Lark and his unsuccessful attempt at blue jay negotiations that tears began streaming down our faces and our stomachs began to ache.

"Did it work? Did they eventually stop?" I asked wiping my eyes, trying to control my laughter.

"Of course, it didn't work," she snorted. "I think they chased after him a quarter of a mile before eventually losing interest and turning around." She smiled at the memory, "Oh, my gosh, he was so mad at me for just standing there and watching, but what was I supposed to do, he was the bird aficionado, after all."

"What ever happened to Lark?" asked Grandma Helen.

"I think he teaches ornithology at Cornell University, or at least he did the last time I spoke with him," answered mom.

"Orni-what?" I asked.

"Ornithology," said mom, "it's essentially the study of birds." She picked her phone up off the counter, "You know, I'm actually still friends with him on Facebook, so why don't we just take a moment to see what our little bird enthusiast is up to now?" She silently scrolled through her phone and then shouted out unexpectedly, "Oh, my God! You are never going to believe this."

"What?" we asked simultaneously.

"Well, apparently, Lark Owens has found love with a member of the *Washing Well Wenches*," said mom.

"I'm sorry, what exactly is that dear?" asked Grandma Helen.

"It's basically an all-female comedy show where they dress as milkmaids and do a lot of improv and comedy skits."

"Ooh, now that sounds intriguing," said Grandma Helen excitedly. "Maybe that's something we should think about bringing to the theater."

"At Renaissance Festivals," added mom mischievously.

"Ugh, you just had to ruin it, didn't you? You know how I feel about outdoor entertainment, Olivia, and Renaissance Festivals are simply abhorrent."

"How would you know; you've never even been to one?" asked mom.

"I have a television, dear, and I see the incessant advertisements every spring." She curled her lip, "It's truly sad that those people have nothing better to do than traipse lazily around a cow pasture all day looking dreadful and severely hygienically challenged. I mean honestly, what is so appealing about attending a festival that celebrates filthiness while eating turkey legs and drinking beer?"

"Ale," said mom.

"What?" she asked.

"It's called ale at the festivals," clarified mom.

"Let's not get into semantics, Olivia," she said. "I don't care if it's ale, beer, or pig swill, it's all unrefined and uncouth, if you ask me."

"Yes, well, we didn't," said mom. "Anyway, Lark is now travelling with his new friends and is also the featured expert at the Birds of Prey exhibit." She looked back down at her phone, "And, he and his fiancé 'Pack-a-Punch Petunia,' will apparently be getting married during the Knights of the Roundtable jousting show next month in Poughkeepsie."

Grandma Helen and I stared silently back at mom until the three of us simultaneously broke out in a raucous laughter.

"Oh, my gosh, mom, that could have been you had you played your cards right," I snickered.

"Yes, well, as much as I would love to travel around the country drinking ale and eating turkey legs, I think your grandmother would have an absolute conniption knowing that her youngest daughter was not only living the life of a nomad, but also carousing with lascivious outdoor thespians," said mom.

Grandma Helen finished the last of her wine, stood up, and kissed me on the cheek, "I'm glad you had fun on your date, darling." She then took her wine glass, placed it in the sink, and looked over at mom, "And conniption doesn't even begin to describe the wrath and ire that would be emitting from the very core of my being if you ever pulled a stunt like that, my dear."

19

"That sounds somewhat ominous," said mom uneasily.

"Well, don't ever become an ignominious travelling carnival act, and you'll never have to worry about finding out what that means." She smiled brightly, "Alright, well, it's time for me to catch up on my beauty sleep, so I suppose it's time for me to retire. Goodnight, my darlings!"

"You know, it's really unnerving how she can look so sweet and unassuming on the outside, while encapsulating a wrath that could literally rival the force of an entire army on the inside," said mom.

"Yeah, I'm betting she could probably give Pack-a-Punch Petunia a run for her money," I said.

"Honey, that woman could probably give Mike Tyson a run for his money." She put the remnants of the charcuterie back in the refrigerator and turned her attention back to me, "So, how did the date really go?"

"Just like I said, he was wonderful, kind, and treated me like a lady." I wiped down the kitchen counter and then paused to look at her, "I really like this one, mom."

"Oh, honey, that makes me so happy." She started to pull me in for a hug and then stopped abruptly, "Wait, you do plan on bringing him around the family so that we can meet him, yes? I really don't want to have to endure another game of keep-away, like I am with Ezra."

"Actually, I was thinking about inviting him over for the tree trimming on Friday," I smiled sheepishly.

"Oh, that would be wonderful, honey, we would love to have him join us." she picked up the box of crackers and put them in the pantry, "You're not worried that it's too early to have him come to something like that? A family gathering, I mean?"

"We've been dating over a month, so yeah, I think it's okay," I said.

"Well, I for one am really looking forward to meeting this boy." She folded the kitchen towel and hugged me goodnight, "By the way, you may want to prepare him for the tsunami that is your grandmother. I don't even want to begin thinking about the horrendous things that will inevitably be exiting her mouth." She turned and started toward her bedroom, "Honestly, I think we should start offering up prayer now."

"I couldn't agree more, mom," I mumbled as I cut out the light.

CHAPTER FOUR

Later the next morning, I came downstairs to find mom rummaging through Christmas boxes that had been strategically placed in each corner of the living room.

"Where is he?" she mumbled to herself, "I know I packed him away in this box, so he should be right here."

"What are you looking for?" I asked.

"Alfie." She put her hands on her hips and scanned the room, "I can't seem to find him anywhere and I know I packed him in the box with all the mantle decorations."

Alfie is our Elf on the Shelf that mom insists on bringing back each Christmas, even though she knows full well that we all know the truth about Santa. She claims some of her happiest Christmases were due to Alfie and his magical ability to tame the three of us into submission, but if I'm being completely honest, this unceremonious compliance came at a high cost to both her mental well-being and late-night wine consumption. You see, Alfie brought a reprieve to the incessant sibling rivalry and obnoxiousness, yes, but he also brought stress and chaos to our mother during his brief seasonal stay. So, while my brothers and I were honored to be hosting one of Santa's most prestigious and informative elves over the holidays, our mother was left to contend with the nightly responsibility of moving Alfie around the house or the daily responsibility of coming up with creative and logical reasons as to why he hadn't. It was also during this time that she came to the realization that wine and elf duty, despite her many failed attempts, did not necessarily complement one another, and that Alfie, regardless of his high station at the North Pole, was a great big pain in the ass.

"Have you had your morning coffee yet?" I asked skeptically.

"Yes, why?" she stopped rummaging to look up at me.

"Well, you may want to think about having another cup because he's sitting right over there." I pointed over to Churchill's dog bed. "I don't know about you, but I'm thinking this may be a new development in their relationship."

She turned around to see Churchill, our English Bulldog, quietly humping poor Alfie. "Churchill, no!" She ran over and grabbed the doll from under him, "Why do you insist on humping things that don't belong to you? We've discussed this!"

"He's a dog, mom," I offered pragmatically.

"Yes, but that doesn't mean he should take things that don't belong to him; besides I gave him a special pillow to do that with." She bent down to dote on him, "I thought you and Ms. Fluffy were happy together, or you at least seemed to be yesterday." She pulled the pillow closer to him, "She's right here if you need her, baby."

"You need help," I said.

Ignoring the slight, she walked into the kitchen, "Why don't you go ahead and give Churchill a treat while I clean Alfie?"

"A treat?" I asked incredulously, "but you just scolded him."

"I know, but he looks so sad and lonely now, and he needs to know that we still love him." She dampened a towel, "He's a very sensitive animal and needs to be reassured of our love."

"Have you met him? He ignores everyone in this family, including you." I grabbed a treat from the canister, "You really need to stop deluding yourself into thinking that dog loves you as much as you love him."

"Mom! Mom!" interrupted Beau as he ran down the stairs, "I need your help with this problem!"

"I'm right here, Beau, you don't need to shout," she said.

"Oh, sorry, I wasn't sure where you were." He sidled up next to her and plopped his math book on the counter, "I can't figure out this problem."

She gestured toward the kitchen table silently telling him to have a seat, "I'll be right with you, I just need to put Alfie somewhere he won't be molested."

"What's this?" I mocked, "you're actually going to deprive your poor sweet baby of finding love?" I handed Churchill his treat, "He may never forgive you for that."

"Hence, the treat." She looked down at the red elf in her hands, "Also, Alfie never signed up to be a canine love slave, so I think it's best that we just keep them separated for now."

"Why do you still bring Alfie out every Christmas, anyway?" asked Beau. He watched her walk into the living room, "I mean, we all know the truth now, so why even bother?"

"Nostalgia, I suppose." She placed Alfie on the mantle and then walked back over to the table where Beau was sitting, "And perhaps I keep holding onto the hope that he will somehow still motivate you to behave," she winked at him.

"Hey, I behave!" he said disparagingly.

She stared silently back at him, one eyebrow arched.

"Okay, well, attempts have been made," he conceded.

She looked down at the math problem in his notebook, "Beau, honey, you know the answer to this one."

"That's not the one I'm talking about," he said.

"I understand but does this really look like the correct answer for this particular problem?" she asked.

"Yes, it's 30/6," he said confidently.

"Honey, what is the number one rule when working with fractions?" She reached for her coffee sitting on the counter, "What is it that I always tell you to do?"

"Reduce them to their lowest form."

"Exactly, always reduce them." She pointed to the paper, "Now, having that information readily at the forefront of your mind, do you still think that 30/6 is the correct answer?"

He looked down at his paper and nodded, "Yes."

"Beau, you do remember that fractions can sometimes turn into whole numbers, yes?" she asked.

"Yeah, I know," he said.

"Okay, then what is the answer?" she tried again.

"30/6," he repeated.

"How is it that you're not understanding what I'm saying?" She pointed to the paper again, "What is the answer, son?"

"Well, I'm beginning to sense that it's not 30/6," he grumbled.

"No, Beau it's not." She took off her reading glasses, rubbed her eyes, and took a deep breath, "Please, just look at it again and tell me if you can reduce it anymore."

"Oh, I see it now," he said excitedly, "the answer's five."

"Yes, that is correct," she said.

"Yes, thank you, God!" he exclaimed. "I was seriously worried I was going to have to sit here all day doing this, so I'm super glad I dodged that bullet."

Mom sighed audibly and took a few moments to gather her wits, "Okay, what is the other problem you're having trouble with?"

"Oh, this one." He pointed at the page, "It says the answer is one thing, but I'm literally getting the opposite answer."

She looked over his shoulder at the problem, "No, you've got the correct answer, it's a negative nine."

"Well, it says it's a positive nine in the back of the book," he said.

"It does?" She grabbed his notebook and a dry erase marker and walked over to the white board mounted on the wall, "Let's go ahead and write it on the board and see if we can figure out what's going on."

"Do I have to sit here while you do this?" he asked.

"Considering this is your problem that I am trying to help you with, yes." She wrote the problem down, worked it out, and came up with the same answer as Beau. "Hmm, this doesn't make any sense, this should be a negative nine, not a positive nine." She turned back to Beau, "Are you sure you wrote the problem down correctly?"

He looked down at his book and then back up at the board and nodded, "Yes."

She reworked the problem again, and again, got the same answer, "Please tell me I'm not crazy, there isn't supposed to be a parenthesis here, correct?"

"Ugh, I really don't care," he groaned, "I just want to be done."

"Seriously, this doesn't make any sense." She continued to scrutinize the problem, "A negative three squared not in parenthesis is a negative nine, not a positive nine."

"I don't care, mom," he rolled his eyes. "Will you please just let me go on to the next problem so that I can get this over with?"

"You should want to figure this out, Beau." She put her hands on her hips and looked at him sternly, "It's important to keep problem solving whenever the answer doesn't reveal itself to you right away because it shows that you are not only tenacious and persistent, but also unwilling to accept defeat."

"Oh, I'm totally willing to accept defeat," he said casually, "especially if it means I don't have to spend all day figuring out things like that," he referenced the white board.

"Beau, honey, you're a smart boy, math doesn't have to be your Achilles heel," she said.

"Yes, well, it's a known fact that four out of every three people struggle with math, so I think I'll just stick with what I know." He grinned mischievously, "Did you catch my joke? Four out of every three people? I crack myself up!"

Yes, I am well acquainted with that joke," she smiled, "and it's not one of your better ones, so let's just try to figure this out, shall we?" She picked up her marker and reworked the problem while Beau looked on in a state of complete tedium, "Okay, so we bring the negative three squared that is not in parenthesis down, and since it is not in parenthesis, it becomes a negative nine, right?" She raised her hands in frustration, "I don't get it, I've done everything right, how is this a positive nine?" She looked over at Beau and waved her hand in front of his face, "Hello, earth to Beau, have you even been paying attention?"

"Yes," he drawled out irritably.

"No, you haven't, you've sat here and let me do all the work." She pointed back toward the board, "Do you happen to have any thoughts as to what's going on here?"

"Ugh, fine!" He tossed his head back in frustration, "You want to know what I think happened? I think that when Thanos snapped his fingers, the negative sign wasn't lucky enough to be taken away like the rest of humanity, and now thrives on making people miserable."

Mom stared silently back at him for a few seconds before speaking, "Are you referring to the Thanos from the Marvel movies?"

"Maybe," he smiled sheepishly.

She continued staring at him, not quite sure how to respond, and then laughed out heartily, "Okay, now that was funny."

She lovingly mussed his hair and kissed him on the forehead, "Listen, I'll keep working on this to see if I can figure out where we might be going wrong, but I still want you to go ahead and finish the rest of the problems, okay?"

"Okay, I will" he said and grabbed his books off the table, "You know, mom, the only real difference between those two answers is a negative sign, so I wouldn't even worry about it." He turned toward his room, "It's like I always say, as long as it's close enough for government work, you don't really need to worry, because those people get away with everything."

Mom stared after him incredulously, "And who told you that?"

"Dad," he called out.

"Well, he does have a point, I suppose." She turned her attention back to the problem at hand, "Addie, do you see where I'm going wrong with this?"

"It looks right to me, mom." I walked over to her, "Textbooks are not infallible, so maybe it's just a mistake or a typo." I grabbed a banana from the fruit bowl sitting on the counter, "Hey, I still have some history to read over, so do you mind if I just take this up to my room?"

"That's fine honey," she said distractedly.

She spent another ten minutes trying to decipher the elusive algebraic riddle before finally giving up, erasing the board, and pouring herself another cup of coffee. She then walked back into the living room and noticed Churchill sprawled out on his bed atop Ms. Fluffy, slumbering peacefully despite his licentious morning tryst with Alfie.

"You definitely have eclectic taste, my dear; I'll give you that." She pulled his blanket over him, "And don't worry, I don't think Alfie will rat you out to Santa, but you may want to be extra nice to mommy just in case."

She then went back to rummaging through the Christmas boxes and was decorating the mantle when Aunt Christine walked through the back door.

"Good morning, dear sister!" she exclaimed.

"It's definitely a morning," said mom.

"Uh oh," said Aunt Christine placing her purse and keys on the counter. She walked into the living room, peered over the mess currently littering the floor and asked, "So, are we drinking coffee or wine this morning?"

Mom immediately placed the nutcracker she was holding back in its box and headed toward the kitchen, "Wine sounds like a good idea to me."

"Yay!" exclaimed Aunt Christine, "I love being reminded that I'm not the only lush in the family."

Chapter Five

Aunt Christine pulled open the refrigerator, grabbed the chardonnay and poured two glasses, "Not to be one to point out the obvious, but don't you think you should have started on all of this a couple of weeks ago?" She handed mom a glass and leaned against the kitchen counter, "I mean, it's already December 10th, and your tree isn't even up yet."

"Yes, well, educating my children and dealing with the cyclone that is our mother tends to keep me a tad bit busy these days." She looked past Aunt Christine and into the dining room where a large rectangular box sat, "Besides, I'm planning on having the boys put the tree up later today, and then of course Friday, we'll happily come together as a family to decorate it." She sipped her wine, "The kids are really looking forward to it."

"Are they really?" she asked.

"No," she said.

"You know, I just finished the edits for my Hong Kong shoot, so if you'd like me to, I can help you with some of the decorating." She looked over at the mess currently blanketing the living room, "You definitely need help, and it's the least I can do considering you and Greg are giving me free room and board until I can find a place of my own."

Seven months ago, during the celebration of Grandma Helen's birthday week, Aunt Christine made the surprising proclamation that she was planning on moving out of her SoHo apartment in order to move back home to be closer to family. Being a freelance photographer has allowed her the freedom to live wherever she wants, and for some inane reason, at least according to Grandma Helen, she wants to live here, in Georgia. So now, when she's not traversing the globe photographing exotic locales, she's either checking out the local market for real estate, spending time with her boyfriend, Brian, or helping to keep tabs on Grandma Helen, which, as we all know, is a full-time job.

"I'd really appreciate the help, thank you," said mom gratefully.

"Hey, what do you say we grab this bottle, take it into the living room and make it look like a cheesy Hallmark Christmas movie?" asked Aunt Christine.

"I think that sounds like a great idea." Mom picked up her glass and headed into the living room, "I've already started on the mantle, but you can go ahead and set up the nativity, if you want."

"Okay, just let me grab one more thing." She popped into the pantry and brought out the giant bag of peanut M&M's mom hides from the rest of the family, "I figured since we don't have any Christmas goodies yet, we'll have to make do with these."

"Wait a minute, how do you know where I stash those? Nobody even knows I have them," said mom.

"Please, Ollie, you're nothing if not predictable," she sauntered confidently over to her and held out the bag, "and everyone knows you have them."

"I feel violated," said mom grabbing a handful of candy, "and not in good way."

"Well, if it makes you feel any better, little sis, I was completely violated last night, and it was most certainly in a good way," winked Aunt Christine.

"Thank you for that lovely visual as we enter into this season of celebration at the birth of our Lord and Savior," said mom sarcastically.

She picked up the nutcracker she had set down earlier, "Speaking of Brian, is he mentally preparing himself for the impending family festivities this Friday?"

Brian Caldwell, air marshal, avid hiker, and all-around good guy, is an old childhood crush of Aunt Christine's who unexpectedly ran into her while she was visiting last May. The two of them hit it off immediately, in more ways than one, and have been inseparable ever since. More importantly, Brian has received the elusive Grandma Helen seal of approval and has been extended a regular invite to all Sunday family night dinners, which is practically unheard of. I've got to hand it to Aunt Christine because she primed him perfectly. She taught him how to speak Grandma Helen's love language, so the moment he went out of his way to attend not one, but three of her performances of *Oklahoma* and willingly played Kenny Rogers to her Sheena Easton in the duet, *We've Got Tonight,* at one of her weekly karaoke nights, she was completely smitten. This newfound admiration, however, has caused a few minor kinks in the form of constant pestering about wedding dates, themes, and colors, but considering the alternative, Aunt Christine is more than happy to appease her, even though neither she nor Brian have ever mentioned the idea of getting married.

"He's really looking forward to it, especially since his family doesn't do much to celebrate Christmas," said Aunt Christine.

"Are they Jewish?" asked mom.

"No, they're just older," she said. "I guess since he's an only child and they don't have any grandchildren, they prefer not to deal with the hassle of decorating." She unwrapped a large wooden stable, "Where do you want me to set up the Nativity?"

"You can put it right here," said mom making room on the living room table. "That sounds so depressing. Do they at least have a tree?"

"No tree, no wreathes, no garland, no festive inclinations whatsoever." Aunt Christine placed the manger on the table, "They apparently just sit around the kitchen on Christmas morning and hand each other gift cards." She then unwrapped the baby Jesus and laid him in the manger, "They aren't the most affectionate family either, so he really enjoys spending time with ours. He thinks mom is great, by the way, he loves her zest for life."

"Zest? Is that what we're calling it now?" Mom stopped what she was doing and looked over at Christine, "He obviously hasn't experienced her at full volume yet."

"Good morning, my darlings!" Grandma Helen strolled casually through the back door making her way to the kitchen in search of coffee. "I see you're finally bringing the spirit of Christmas into this house," she pulled a mug from the cupboard, "I was beginning to think that you'd forgotten."

"Good morning, mother," care to help us?" asked mom.

"Not particularly, dear, no." She poured coffee into her mug and sighed heavily, "Besides, I need to go and itemize a list of all the toys and other merchandise needed to fulfill the Angel Tree obligations that the theater is sponsoring." She sipped her coffee, "It's tedious work, but it is for charity."

"Wait, you're doing something charitable?" asked mom.

"For others?" clarified Aunt Christine.

Before Grandma Helen had a chance to respond, her phone rang, "Oh, it's Joan, I'd better take this." She swiped to answer before putting the phone to her ear, "Good morning, darling, how are you this glorious day?"

"Hi Helen, I'm so sorry to bother you, I hope I'm not interrupting anything," said Joan frantically.

"No, you're not interrupting anything, I'm just helping my daughters decorate the house for Christmas," she said gleefully.

"Oh, well, I'll make this quick, then," said Joan.

"Before you do, just give me one second," interrupted Grandma Helen. She muted the call, sipped her coffee, and casually surveyed her nails, "Olivia, do you still have some of that hazelnut coffee creamer?"

"What are you doing, mother?" asked mom in confusion.

"I'm pretty sure that something unpleasant is about to be asked of me, so I'm just making her squirm for a little bit." She peeked into the refrigerator, grabbed the creamer and added it to her coffee. She then waited another few seconds before clearing her throat and unmuting the call, "Sorry about that, darling, I had to stop Olivia from making a huge decorating faux pax. The poor girl tries so hard to be domestic but is rarely successful."

"That woman needs to be committed," grumbled mom.

"Oh, I understand completely," said Joan. "Decorating can be a lot of work, that's why I love it whenever my grandkids come over to help me. We decorate the tree, make cookies, string popcorn, sing Christmas carols," she paused briefly, "it's such a magical time filled with wonder and excitement!"

"I'm sure you think it is, dear," said Grandma Helen. "So, to what do I owe the honor of this lovely and unexpected morning phone call?"

"Oh yes, I'm sorry, I guess I got a little off track there." She took a deep breath before continuing, "Helen, I'm in dire need of a favor. I'm in over my head and I think you're the only person that can help me right now."

"I find that is often the case, dear," soothed Grandma Helen. "Tell me, what is it that you need?"

"Well, you remember how I volunteered to organize the Toys for Tots charity drive and shop for the Angel Tree gifts?" asked Joan.

"Yes, I do," said Grandma Helen rolling her eyes. "It would seem as though you're giving Mother Teresa a run for her money this year."

"Oh, you are so sweet to say that, thank you," said Joan, ignorant to the sarcasm behind the statement. "Anyway, my daughter just reached out to me asking for help with the local women's shelter, so now between helping her and trying to organize the Toys for Tots, I'm completely swamped, and have no time to do the shopping for the Angel Tree. And since you already have the wish lists of all the recipients, I was hoping you might be willing to go and do the shopping for me," she paused and then added desperately, "I would be forever in your debt, Helen, I really would."

"Forever in your debt." Four words that are practically music to Grandma Helen's ears. Whereas you and I, or any normal person for that matter, might acknowledge these words as a plea for help, Grandma Helen looks at them as an opportunity, something to keep in her back pocket for future exploit. So, while Joan may not have known it at the time, she had just unwittingly offered herself as sacrifice to the one person who has no qualms cashing in on any favor made during a personal crisis.

"I see, well, I suppose a little extra shopping time at Nordstrom and Macy's won't interfere too much with my hectic schedule," she picked a piece of lint from her pant leg, "I figure it's the least I can do having been blessed with so much in my own life."

"Umm, Helen, we don't really have the budget to shop in those stores, so I'm thinking you may want to set your sights a little bit lower," said Joan.

"Oh, okay, well, I guess I can head over to The Mill and do my shopping there," she appeased. "They always have the cutest little shops, and the best espresso bar in town, so that should work out just fine."

"I was actually thinking more along the lines of Walmart," said Joan hesitantly.

"Walmart?" she shrieked. "You want me to shop at Walmart?"

"We can get so much more for our money there and they carry a lot of the necessities these people are needing, so it only makes sense," soothed Joan. "And I'll even give you my credit card so that you won't have to use your own money and wait to be reimbursed."

"I hate Walmart, Joan, you know this," said Grandma Helen.

"I know, and I promise I'll make it up to you," consoled Joan.

"Ugh, do I have to?" she pouted.

"Think about all the families counting on us right now, Helen," she pleaded. "They have nothing, and this small gesture would mean the absolute world to them."

"Eh, I guess," she conceded.

"And think about all the children you'll be bringing happiness and joy to," continued Joan. "They'll be able to experience all the magic of Christmas and delight in the knowledge that Santa didn't forget them this year."

"Eh, yeah," she said weakly.

"And Tobias reached out to his reporter friend over at WXBTV and…"

"I'll do it!" she cried out exuberantly.

CHAPTER SIX

"Girls, I'm going to be on TV!" trumpeted Grandma Helen giddily as she set down her phone. "Joan just filled me in on everything, and I am beyond ecstatic!"

"That's great mom!" cheered Aunt Christine.

"That's fantastic, I'm so happy for you," said mom. "How did all of this come about?"

"Well, apparently Tobias has a friend who is a reporter for WXBTV, and she is planning on bringing her news crew to the theater when we pack up the boxes for the Angel Tree, and since I am now in charge of the Angel Tree, I will be the one that they interview." She clapped her hands enthusiastically, "Oh, this is so exciting!"

"We're really excited for you too, mom," said Aunt Christine.

"Wait, so you're in charge of the Angel Tree now?" asked mom. "I thought Joan was overseeing all of that."

"She was, dear, but it seems that she has spread herself rather thin with organizing both the Toys for Tots drive and helping her daughter with the women's shelter, so now it's incumbent upon me to have to pick up the rest of her slack."

"That's a rather harsh way of putting it, don't you think?" asked mom. "Joan has been spending a lot of her own time and money trying to get things in order for both charities, with little to no help from you, I might add, so you may want to show her some grace and not be so rude about it."

"The woman is making me shop at Walmart, Olivia, so no, I don't think it's too harsh," retorted Grandma Helen. "Besides, had the board opted to go with my idea of the telethon, she wouldn't be needing to spread herself so thin, and I would be preparing my introductory monologue for millions of viewers."

Each Christmas the theater chooses one or two local charities to sponsor, so when the board met during their last quarterly meeting, they spent much of the time deliberating over what to do and which charity to support. Joan and a few other members nominated the Angel Tree and Toys for Tots, while Grandma Helen pitched the idea of a televised telethon. Despite her enthusiasm and selfless willingness to play host, the board turned her down, citing the inaccessibility of funds needed to put on such a production and the unnecessary extravagance that comes with bringing an event like that to small town Georgia. This, of course, then served as a catalyst for Grandma Helen's complete lack of enthusiasm in offering any aid, beyond what was expected, to her good friend, Joan, and outright animosity to the board that had so rudely denied her.

"I think you might be overestimating the theater's reach with that number, mom," said Aunt Christine. She placed a lid on one of the empty boxes and moved it out of the way. "Besides, the donations coming in are double what they were last year, and that is in large part due to Joan and all of her efforts, so maybe you should consider letting her be a part of all of this with you."

"Yes, I understand that, dear, but I'm the one overseeing the Angel Tree now, so it only makes sense that I be the one interviewed!" she said tersely.

"We understand that you want to be on TV, mom, but if you were truly being honest with yourself, you'd see that Joan is really the one that should be interviewed when WXBTV comes to town," said mom.

"Did neither one of you hear what I said earlier? I have to go to Walmart!" she shrilled. "That in and of itself is an incredibly charitable act on my part, so it's only right that I get some recognition too."

"I don't think that's how charity is supposed to work, mom," said Aunt Christine.

"Well, it should," bristled Grandma Helen.

"You know, maybe you and Joan could do the interview together; that way everybody wins," smiled mom.

"Listen, Joan said that if I did this favor for her, she would be more than happy to let me do the interview. Besides, I'm much better at impromptu speaking, even Joan says so." She picked up the baby Jesus and carefully studied over it, "Of course, having Joan and I both do the interview would give us an opportunity to discuss all three charities, which could very well lead to even more donations for next year, thus enabling us to help even more people."

"There you go, mom, that's the spirit," said Aunt Christine.

Grandma Helen looked over at them with a gleam in her eye, "And by continuing to reach out to more people in need, we can grow even bigger and make this a yearly opportunity where we invite even more reporters to cover our story." She set down the baby Jesus and excitedly cried out, "Oh, girls, this is brilliant! I'm going to be on every news station in Atlanta!"

"Wait, what just happened?" asked mom.

"I was thinking too small, that's what happened," said Grandma Helen. She glanced over at the clock above the kitchen, "Listen, it's getting late, and I can't continue to dawdle over here; not with everything I need to do now." She poured herself more coffee and looked imploringly over at mom, "Olivia, darling, would you be a dear and come with me to Walmart, I really don't want to have to face that terror alone."

"It's amazing how sweet you can be when you want something, mother." She began to hang stockings over the fireplace, "Why don't we plan for Thursday?"

"Wonderful!" she exclaimed happily. "Alright, well, I'm off to play Santa and write Christmas lists for poor little boys and girls!"

"Wow, I'm not exactly sure what just happened there, but something seemed to perk her up," said Aunt Christine.

"Yes, well, rather than having visions of sugar-plums dancing in her head, that woman has television news reporters crowding around a lectern podium," answered mom.

The two of them continued to decorate and make small talk about the upcoming family Christmas gathering when mom suddenly looked up and said, "Hey, what do you say we play a joke on mom and put coal in her stocking this year?"

"Have you lost your mind; she'd kill you and then set me up with the evidence," said Aunt Christine.

"Oh, come on, I think it would be funny," laughed mom.

"Oh no, I'm not letting you drag me down that rabbit hole, I know better." She wound a strand of lighted garland around the front stairwell,

"And as much as I would love to play Bonnie to your Clyde, being a corpse does not align itself with my New Year's Eve plans this year, so I'm afraid I'm going to have to pass."

"Spoil sport." Mom stacked two boxes of Christmas ornaments in the corner and snapped her fingers excitedly, "Oh, wait, I know, we could have one of those personalized Santa videos made where he notifies her that she's on the naughty list due to poor behavior and selfish inclinations."

"I think she would kill you in your sleep and make me watch," said Aunt Christine.

"We could send it anonymously; she wouldn't even know," conspired mom. "Come on, Chrissy, don't be a wuss."

Aunt Christine wound another strand of garland around the other handrail, quietly contemplating the pros and cons of early death, "You know, if we get caught, I'm going to throw you under the bus so fast it'll make your head spin."

"Noted," said mom.

Aunt Christine secured the garland to the handrail and began attaching small red bows, "I don't know, Ollie, it seems kind of immature." She looked over at mom, "I mean we're grown women; don't you think we're a little old to be playing tricks on our mother?"

"Chrissy, do you remember the time mom told everyone about your first gynecological visit? How you passed out after seeing the speculum, clamp, and forceps lying on the table and then describing in detail how you freaked out because the leftover lubricant made you think you were leaking?"

"Okay, that was a long time ago, and looking back on it now, it was a rather funny story," she laughed.

"It really was funny," snickered mom. "I remember you being convinced the doctor had actually punctured your uterus and that you were going to die a virgin. Mom had to buy you three large scoops of chocolate peanut butter ice cream doused in whipped cream to finally get you to calm you down."

"Yes, well, I remember you benefited from that trip to Baskin and Robbins as well, so you're welcome." She attached the last red bow to the garland, "And who could ever forget the time she procrastinated too long in reading *Jane Eyre* for her book club, and rather than own up to it, she lied and said that you had contracted a tapeworm after eating homemade tamales at your friend, Rosalita's house."

"Oh God, I remember that!" said mom. "And then she told all the ladies in the group she was too consumed with worry to focus on reading, when in truth, she had just gotten bored after the second page."

Mom flanked the fireplace with two artificial poinsettias "You know, mom is not above reproach, so I think we're perfectly entitled to have a little fun at her expense."

"Okay, fine, you talked me into it," smiled Aunt Christine. "I mean, it's not like one of us is going to wake up with a bloody horse's head in their bed or a boiling bunny on the stove, right?"

"Well, considering both of those scenarios would require her to work with animals, I'm thinking we're safe," laughed mom.

An hour later, once the decorating was finished and the bottle of wine empty, the two of them were sitting around mom's laptop laughing uncontrollably as they typed a rather large list of complaints and grievances onto the "Santa is Watching You" website mom had used when we were younger. Beau and I could hear their raucous laughter from upstairs, so it was no wonder they didn't hear us coming into the kitchen for lunch.

"Hey, wait a minute, I recognize that Santa," said Beau walking over to the computer. "He's the one that told me that if I helped mom take out the trash and do my schoolwork without complaint, I'd be on the nice list and finally get the Lego Millennium Falcon I'd been asking for."

"You know, now that you mention it, I think he's the same one that told me to stop leaving my soccer cleats in the house or face being on the naughty list for the first time in my life," I added.

"I think he's also the one that told Ezra that if he didn't stop sneaking food upstairs, he would fill his stocking with Brussel sprouts and bean curd," said Beau.

"Bean curd?" laughed Aunt Christine, "that's certainly one I haven't heard before."

"Let me tell you something," said mom, "this man is a godsend to parents everywhere," Greg and I were able to enjoy a whole month of peace and tranquility for only $20, which is an absolute steal, when you're dealing with three children under the age of 10."

"Who are you making this video for, anyway?" I asked.

"Oh, your mother and I just thought we'd have a little fun and make one to send to your grandmother as a little Christmas joke," said Aunt Christine.

"Oh, this is going to be good," said Beau, "I can't wait to tell Ezra!"

"No, this can't go beyond this room," said mom. "The less people that know about this, the better."

"Why?" asked Beau.

"Because we're sending it anonymously," said Aunt Christine.

"Smart," nodded Beau knowingly. "Self-preservation is always a smart idea, especially wherever Grandma Helen is concerned."

"Do you really think Grandma is petty enough to get upset over something like this? Surely, she can take a joke," I said.

"That woman's the definition of petty, of course she's going to be upset," said Ezra walking into the kitchen.

"Ezra, I didn't even hear you come in," said mom.

"No one ever does unless I want them to," he deadpanned, "I'm like a ninja." He grabbed an apple from the refrigerator and bit into it, "So, what's going on?"

"Can I tell him, mom, please?" begged Beau.

"Okay, fine," sighed mom, "but you can't say anything, Ezra, you have to promise me."

"I'm pretty sure the NSA already knows all our secrets, mom, so if they haven't come after you yet, I'm thinking you're safe from the tin foil, at least for now," said Ezra sarcastically.

"Yes, well, your grandmother doesn't, and she most certainly will, so let's just go ahead and plan to keep all of this under wraps, okay?" asked mom.

Ezra quietly ate his apple and listened intently as Beau filled him in on the plan to Santa shame Grandma Helen. Once Beau had finished explaining everything, he laughed out heartily and said, "It's certainly original, I'll give you that." He walked into the kitchen to throw away the remnants of his apple, "So, when are you planning on sending it?"

"We haven't gotten that far," said Aunt Christine.

"Well, you may want to consider covering your tracks before you do," he said.

"We all know your grandmother isn't the most computer savvy person, so I highly doubt she'll be able to track who sent it," said mom. "Besides, it was only two days ago that she found out she needed to close the open tabs on her computer to make it run faster, so I'm thinking tracking an email is slightly out of her wheelhouse."

"Wow, how many tabs did she have open to make it run so slow?" I asked.

"124," she sighed, "and that was only after I started counting."

CHAPTER SEVEN

After lunch, Beau and I went back to our schoolwork, Ezra went upstairs to his room, and mom and Aunt Christine continued to hash out whether or not to send the Santa shaming video to Grandma Helen.

"I just think it may be wise to sit on it for a while, that's all," said Aunt Christine. "Maybe keep it in our back pocket for a bit."

"I suppose you're right," said mom. "I certainly don't want to hurt her feelings, but sometimes that woman asks for it, you know?"

"Well, she's not the most affable person in the world, so it's easy to want to put her in her place." Aunt Christine grabbed a mug from the cabinet, "I'm going to make myself a cup of coffee, would you like one?"

"That sounds delightful, thank you," said mom. She picked up her phone and began scrolling through her multiple Christmas lists, "So, have you decided what you're going to get Brian for Christmas yet?"

"We've decided not to give each other gifts this year and instead are planning on taking a romantic ski vacation together." She scooped hazelnut coffee into a filter and poured water into the coffee maker, "Of course, we've also talked about going to Spain and Greece, but I think that's going to have to wait until later next year, when our schedules can align for longer trips. So, for now we've just decided to keep it simple by taking more local excursions and being content in knowing that we're able to make special memories together." She poured cream into two mugs, "What about you and Greg?"

"Well, since you asked, we too are planning on making special memories together and have decided to go on an Italian food and wine tour of Tuscany next year. We'll then be heading over to the shores of Portofino to renew our wedding vows, and then follow that up with a quick little trip to Paris to see the Eiffel Tower and the Arc de Triomphe."

"Are you really?" she asked in surprise.

"No, not really," scoffed mom. "We're married with children; we gave up that dream years ago."

"Well, I think you should," she said. "You and Greg will be empty nesters before you know it, so you may want to start thinking about reviving some life back into that dead dream sooner rather than later." She watched as the coffee slowly made its way into the pot, "Besides, you two are both young, healthy, and vital individuals, so why not start making plans now for all the things you'll be able to do once you're not tied down to teaching?"

"I know, you're right." sighed mom, "I guess I just haven't gotten that far yet."

"Of course, I'm right," she winked.

"It's just that if I'm being completely honest, I'd have to admit that I have mixed feelings about all of that. I mean, on the one hand I'm beyond ecstatic because I'll finally be able to do all the things I want to do, but then again on the other hand, I'm not even sure what those things are anymore." She quietly picked at her cuticles, "Somewhere along the way I seemed to have lost sight of who I was before starting this journey, and now the idea of not being able to do it scares me to death." Tears began to form in her eyes, "And what's worse, is I can't help but envision myself coiled up on the floor, bawling my eyes out, just waiting for my adult children to come back home and make me useful again." She wiped away a tear, "It's pathetic, really."

"It's not pathetic, you just love your kids, that's all," said Aunt Christine handing her a tissue. She poured coffee into both of their mugs and set one in front of mom, "You're not the first mother to ever have these feelings, and you certainly won't be the last, so try not to let it get you down."

"That's easier said than done," said mom dabbing at the corners of her eyes.

"Look, you know I applaud everything you've done for your kids. All three of them reflect the love and effort you've poured into them, and all three of them love you and will never forget what you've done for them." She gently took hold of mom's hand, "But, having said that, I definitely think it's time for you to start looking more into your own future and what life will be like for you and Greg once they go off and start their own lives. It's a great big, beautiful world, Ollie, and it's time you start thinking about what comes next…for you."

"You know, Greg and I have actually talked about going to Italy and travelling a good bit more once Beau goes off to college, but as for everything else, I haven't a clue," she shrugged. "I don't want to go back into an office, and I have absolutely no desire to renew my CPA license, so what do I do?"

"You could always write a book," smiled Aunt Christine. "I know that's something that you've always wanted to do, even before you went off to college."

"Yeah, and what would I write about, all of our homeschooling mishaps?"

"Yes, that's exactly what you should write about! That, along with the family dynamics of our well-functioning dysfunctional family, would be more than enough to the fill the pages of a book," she said excitedly. "Hell, mom's antics alone would make for a great story, and Lord knows we have plenty of those."

"Well, I suppose it couldn't hurt to start thinking about my next steps. I mean, who knows, maybe I'll become a big-time author and some movie producer will want to turn my book into a cinematic masterpiece," laughed mom. "Of course, mom will want to play the lead role, but I'm not about to let that happen. I think that should go to either Sandra Bullock or Jennifer Anniston."

"I'm serious, you know." said Aunt Christine. "You're a good writer and you've always been able to make people laugh with your stories, so why not combine the two?"

"I know you are, and I love you for caring enough to tell me all of this," she replied warmly.

Then, in an effort to change the subject and lighten the mood a bit, mom turned the conversation back over to Aunt Christine and Brian's upcoming romantic vacation, "So, where have the two of you decided to go skiing?"

"Well, we're currently looking at Vail, but he's also mentioned Park City, Utah and Jackson Hole, Wyoming. It really doesn't matter to me, I'm honestly fine with either one," she shrugged.

"Have you told him you can't ski yet?" smirked mom.

"Hey, I can ski," she said indignantly, "I just have difficulty staying upright for long periods of time."

"So, what constitutes a long period of time, 10 seconds, because I'm pretty sure that was your record the last time we went skiing," said mom.

"Hey, I've improved since then, thank you very much," she retorted sourly.

"Wait, wasn't that also the time where you fell ass over teakettle while trying to get onto the ski lift?" she laughed. "I honestly have no idea how you were able to flip yourself over, get your ski stuck on the chair, and then hang upside down as the lift continued to move upward. Thank God dad was able to hold onto you long enough for them to reverse the lift and get you down. You were the talk of the ski slope that year, remember?"

"Enjoying this, are you?" asked Aunt Christine.

"Slightly," winked mom.

"Well, for your information, I've already admitted to Brian that I'm a bit of an amateur when it comes to skiing, so you can go ahead and make your little jokes because he's already heard them all. Besides, I'm planning on spending the majority of the time snuggled up by a fire drinking hot toddy's and looking smolderingly sexy, so I highly doubt he'll even be on the slopes long enough to care."

"Just be sure to do the majority of your skiing toward the end of your stay because it's hard to look smolderingly sexy with a broken leg," snickered mom.

Aunt Christine was giving her a one finger salute when Beau walked into the kitchen holding a package. "Mom, I just saw the UPS driver drop this off, and I think it's from your friend in Texas that always sends us Christmas goodies. Can we open it now?"

Mom picked up the box and read the label, "You're right, it is from Lisa." She opened the junk drawer and pulled out a box cutter, "She is always so on top of things, and I always seem to be two steps behind." She paused before opening it, "Guys, this weekend I have to get my baking done, you cannot let me forget, okay?"

"Yes, we'll do that," said Beau hurriedly, "now let's crack this baby open!"

"I've just been so swamped with everything lately, I completely forgot about making them, I hope she understands," fretted mom.

"She'll be fine, mom," he said impatiently.

She opened the package and was barely able to read the card before Beau greedily started opening all the tins, alerting them to what was inside. "Chocolate chip cookies, candy covered almonds, snickerdoodles, gingerbread men…God, I truly love this woman." He then pulled out another bag and opened it, "Mom, she sent us her homemade English muffins too!"

"She makes homemade English muffins?" asked Aunt Christine.

"Oh, my gosh, Aunt Christine, they are the best things you will ever eat, they practically melt in your mouth," he said excitedly.

As Beau continued to hastily unload the sugar-ladened bounty, Mom explained everything to Aunt Christine. "Lisa is a dear friend of mine that used to live down the street from us. When she and her husband, Marcus, moved to Texas a few years ago to be closer to their daughter, she decided to enroll in culinary school and is now a top sous chef at the Ritz in Dallas." She lifted up the large bag, "And Beau's right, these English muffins are to die for."

He picked up a gingerbread man, "You know, it's really sweet that she does this for us, please tell her thank you for me." He bit into the head, "It's always nice to know we can benefit from people liking you."

"Thanks, honey, I think," said mom.

"Please tell me those are from Ms. Lisa and that there's an incredibly large tin of candy covered almonds in there," I said racing into the kitchen. "She said she was going to send extra this year."

"There are, yes, but you're going to have to share with the rest of the family, and more importantly, your father, you know those are his favorite," said mom.

I picked up the tin and held it in front of Aunt Christine, "Would you like some?"

She looked into the tin, grabbed a handful of the multi-colored candy, and popped one into her mouth. Before I had a chance to take some for myself, she quickly grabbed another handful, "Oh my God, those are good."

"Hey mom, I think we should hide everything so we can make it last longer," said Beau picking up a snickerdoodle, "but not in the same place you hide your M&M stash because everyone knows where that is."

Mom immediately looked accusingly over at Aunt Christine.

"I told you everyone knew," she shrugged casually.

"We're not going to do that Beau," said mom. "Besides, Ms. Lisa sent this care package to the whole family, not just a select few, so I don't think she'd take too kindly to us excluding anyone from it."

"Ugh, fine," he grabbed a handful of candied almonds, "But you might want to tell her to up the ante and start doubling down on her cookie production because our family is much too large for such meager offerings."

Before mom had a chance to say anything, dad surprised us all by walking through the back door.

"I'm home!" he called out.

"Great, there go all my snickerdoodles," grumbled Beau irritably.

Dad set down his bags and walked over to us, "Traffic was horrible, I thought I'd never get home."

"I thought you were coming home Thursday," said mom hugging him tightly. "Is everything okay?"

"Everything's fine," he smiled. "I had a customer cancel our meeting tomorrow afternoon, so I just thought I'd come home early and surprise y'all." He peeked over her shoulder, "So, what do we have here?"

"Ms. Lisa sent us her annual Christmas care package, and look, she even sent extra candy covered almonds!" I said lifting the tin.

"Ooh, I love those!" He gave me a quick hug, took a handful of candy, and began perusing over the offerings, "Hold on, are those homemade snickerdoodles?" He grabbed one excitedly, "I love when she makes these!"

"Welp, it was fun while it lasted," said Beau. "I guess I'm going to have to set my sights on the chocolate chip and gingerbread men now."

"It's nice to see you too, son," said dad.

CHAPTER EIGHT

Later that night Grandpa Anthony surprised us all by bringing over dinner. It was an Italian feast full of everything I loved, Fettuccini Alfredo, Bruschetta Focaccia, and his famous Pollo de grandpa, a sauteed chicken breast topped with eggplant, mozzarella, and homemade marinara sauce. He even made pumpkin cheesecake, which after the whole snickerdoodle debacle, made Beau incredibly happy. We were all enjoying a slice when the topic of Grandpa Anthony's motorcycle group came up, a subject that is still a bit of a sore one for Grandma Helen. You see, a few months ago Grandpa Anthony decided to buy a Harley Davidson and join a men's group that rides the mountains of North Georgia every other weekend. When Grandma Helen found out that he had been secretly shopping for a motorcycle, she practically came unglued and even threatened to dance on his grave in tap shoes if he died on one. Since then, she has been slightly more supportive and has even gone so far as to meet a few of his riding buddies, but as for joining them in their bimonthly spousal ride along, she claims that she would rather suffer through an evening of unimaginable hell at the hands of Satan, himself before ever agreeing to mount his two wheeled deathtrap.

"So, Anthony, Olivia tells me that you and the guys are planning on riding as Santa in the downtown Christmas parade, that should be fun," said dad.

"Yeah, we are," he smiled. "We have a bunch of leftover stuffed animals from our visit at the children's hospital, so we thought it would be fun to toss them out to all the kids in the crowd."

"How are you going to carry all of those animals on your motorcycle?" asked Beau. He got up from the table and went to refill his soda, "There can't possibly be enough room."

"We're planning to use the saddle bags we take with us for overnight trips, bud," said Grandpa Anthony.

"No more soda, Beau, you've had plenty," interjected mom.

"What am I supposed to drink, then?" he asked. "My throat is parched."

"Water is great for quenching a parched throat, and there just so happens to be plenty of it in the refrigerator, so please help yourself to a bottle."

"Ugh, you mean the drink that tastes like nothing?" he whined.

"Beau, dear, since you're up, would you please bring me the bottle of chardonnay in the refrigerator?" asked Grandma Helen. She then directed her attention over to Grandpa Anthony, "And when exactly is your little bike club Christmas party again, darling?"

"Next Tuesday," he said.

"Are they still insisting on having it at that godawful barn place?" she asked.

"You know they are, darling," he responded.

"What godawful barn place?" asked Aunt Christine.

"Finger Lickin Good BBQ over in Cartersville," he answered. "Most of the guys live over that way, so we just decided that would be the most convenient place for everyone to meet up."

Finger Lickin Good BBQ is a southern staple here in North Georgia. There are three different locations across the county, and each one is situated inside an old barn decorated to the hilt with rusty farm equipment and enormous walls painted with murals highlighting the day-to-day activities associated with life on a farm. It is the epitome of all things country and serves as a reminder to Grandma Helen of everything she dislikes most about living in the south. On the contrary, it happens to be Nana's favorite restaurant, which is not surprising considering the woman can clean a rib bone like nobody's business and absolutely adores giant pictures of dairy cows eating grass. Anyway, it's country barbeque at its finest, and in no way meets the requirements Grandma Helen deems necessary for a holiday party, regardless of whether or not said party is meant for a group of motorcycle-riding grandpas.

"Ooh, I love good barbeque," cooed Aunt Christine.

"Yes, well, I blame your father for that," mumbled Grandma Helen. "It's unrefined and sticky, I don't know how people can even stand it."

"So, mom said you recently added another member to your group, how is he working out?" asked mom.

"Yes, we did. His name is Rick James, and he's a professor of philosophy over at Kennesaw State University."

"Tell me, is he a jerry curled Super Freak with a penchant for funky high heeled boots?" snickered Ezra.

"Very funny, Ezra, but no, he's not, he's actually quite the opposite," laughed Grandpa Anthony. "He's a good bit younger than the rest of us, but seems to be an old soul, so he's fitting right in."

"Sounds like a fun guy," said Beau sarcastically.

"Oh, Olivia, you may find this interesting, he's actually working on getting his PhD in philosophy, with a specialty in ancient philosophers. In fact, I believe he's doing his thesis on Porphyry, which I thought I overheard you talking to Beau about the other day."

You're right, I was," said mom. "We've been covering quite a few ancient philosophers here lately." She looked over at Beau excitedly, "Pop quiz! True or false, Porphyry once said that man is a featherless biped?"

"Ugh, I hate these," moaned Beau.

"Come on, you know this," she said encouragingly.

"False," he sighed.

"Are you sure about that?" she asked.

"Yes, I am," he stated confidently. "Plato is the one that said man is a featherless biped, while Porphyry is credited with the Porphyrian Tree, which is a classic way to illustrate what is often called a 'scale of being.'"

"Yes, that's correct!" She reached over and hugged him tightly, "Oh, I'm so proud of you, Beau!"

He patted her awkwardly on the back and waited for her to pull away, "Wait, are you crying?" he asked.

"A little bit," she smiled. "I'm just so happy that you were able to answer that without even having to think too hard about it."

"We went over it a few days ago, mom, it hasn't really had time to exit my brain yet," he said.

"Well, we'll just have to keep up with these pop quizzes to make sure it stays in there," she winked.

"Oh yay, more school," he grumbled.

Once dinner was over, mom and I packed away the leftovers and cleaned up the kitchen. I was currently wiping down the table when dad sidled up next to me, "So, I hear you had a date the other night," he said.

"Mom, you told him?" I shrieked.

"Honey, he's coming over Friday to help decorate the tree, I didn't think it would be that big of an issue," said mom defensively.

"So," he nudged my shoulder, "why don't you want me knowing about this Dusty guy?"

"Because I know you're already contemplating what size grave you're going to need to dig," I replied. "Plus, the mental dossier you keep of all my embarrassing moments and less than lady like behavior doesn't elicit much confidence in you acting like a normal person, so you'll have to forgive me for being a bit hesitant."

"Oh, come on, it's all in good fun, honey," he said playfully poking me in the ribs. He pointed at his head and winked, "Besides your brothers fill up twice the space that you do, so who knows, maybe I'll forget a few things."

"Dad, I'm serious, you have to promise me that you'll be nice and won't embarrass me," I said. "He's really looking forward to meeting you and the rest of the family, so please don't make it awkward."

"Sweetheart, I can't wait to meet your boyfriend, and of course I'm going to be nice." He took his glass of bourbon into the living room and laughed heartily, "I'm gonna kill him, but I'm gonna tell him some stories first."

"Dad, please don't!" I turned to mom, "Mom, you can't let him embarrass me, you just can't!"

"Your father's not going to do anything, he's just trying to get a rise out of you," she soothed. "Just ignore him and don't take the bait."

"What's going on?" asked Beau walking into the kitchen.

"Mom and dad have it out for me, that's what's going on," I spat.

"Careful, Addie," warned mom.

"Oh, I see, it's that time of the month again, isn't it?" asked Beau knowingly.

"Shut up, Beau!" I yelled.

"Beau, please stop," said mom calmly.

"This is going to be a disaster mom and you know it! Dusty's going to think we're all insane and run like hell in the other direction the second he has a chance." I looked back over my shoulder, "Between dad with all his embarrassing stories and Grandma Helen's absurd and off-colored remarks, he'll never want to talk to me again." I put my head in my hands, "God, why did I think inviting him was a good idea?"

"Honey, if he's that easily scared away, then he is not worth having in your life," she said.

"You just don't get it, mom," I said. "You and the rest of the family have absolutely no idea how crazy we are compared to everyone else. We're the laughingstock of the neighborhood, and It's humiliating!"

"Listen, you're going to have to get over your little pity party because I've had enough," said mom. "I don't know who you think you are, but you will not give me dirty looks and you most certainly will not speak about your father and grandmother that way."

"She's right, you know, your attitude is not doing you any favors right now," said Beau.

"Would you please stop?" asked mom. "I don't need your help."

"Well, I'm here if you need me," he gently patted her arm.

She pointed over at Beau, "You know, your brother may drive me crazy sometimes, but at least he's respectful while doing it. You, on the other hand, are being completely rude and obnoxious."

"She's right, you know, I really expected more from you, Addie," chimed in Beau.

"Not now, Beau!" blurted mom.

"Yes ma'am." He peered out behind mom and whispered ever so slightly to me, "See?"

"Okay, Beau, please go into the other room with your father," said mom.

"Ugh, fine," he said.

She waited until he was in the other room before continuing, "Look, I understand that you are nervous about Dusty meeting the family, but your dad is not going to embarrass you, I promise. He was just having a little fun at your expense, and if it makes you feel any better, I'll have a talk with him later. As for your grandmother, I will do my best to keep a tight rein on her, but she is who she is, so you may want to forewarn him of what he may be in for."

I took a deep breath to calm myself, "Thanks, mom."

"Everything is going to be okay, so just try to relax," she said.

"I know, and I'm sorry about earlier, I shouldn't have disrespected you." I crossed my arms in front of my chest, "And I'm not really humiliated by our family, I just worry that some people won't understand our familial idiosyncrasies, that's all."

"Honey, I completely understand where you're coming from." She pulled me in for a hug, "Don't forget that I too was a teenager once and that your grandmother was literally breathing down my neck for most of it."

"I can't even begin to imagine what that must have been like." I hugged her tightly, "I love you so much, mom."

"I love you too, baby." She kissed my forehead and then whispered in my ear, "I am curious, though, are you on your period?"

"Ugh, yes," I moaned.

"Well, I guess that makes this outburst a little more understandable, then," she said.

"I'm going to go tell dad I love him and then head upstairs to take a shower. Do you need anymore help?" I asked.

"No, you go on, I've got the rest of this."

As I was making my way into the living room, I passed Beau who was coming back into the kitchen, "I see you're fangs have retracted," he said snidely.

"Shut up, zit face," I said.

"Oh no, they're back," he mocked.

"I hate you," I said.

"I hate you more!"

He strutted into the kitchen directly over to mom, "So, madre, are we still planning to go to the library tomorrow?"

"Yes, we are," she said. "I also need to swing by Nana and Pop's house to pick up some extra cookie tins and then make a quick stop at the dollar store, so you may want to get the majority of your schoolwork finished in the morning, if you can."

"10-4, Kemosabe," he saluted her.

"By the way, you did nothing to help the situation with your sister earlier, I hope you know that." She wiped down the kitchen counter and looked over at him, "Nine times out of ten, it's you that's causing trouble because you stick your nose into business that does not concern you."

"Actually, it's more like one out of ten times," he corrected her.

She stared silently at him, "Like I said, nine times out of ten."

"Minus eight," he grinned.

She folded up the cloth she was using and sighed heavily, "It's true you know, you do drive me crazy, but you also make me laugh." She lovingly moved a few strands of hair from his eyes and hugged him tightly, "I love you so much, you know that right?"

"No, the multiple kisses and constant hugging don't speak to me at all."

Chapter Nine

The next morning, mom and I were downstairs in the kitchen eating breakfast when dad walked in. Mom was intently looking at her phone and typing fervently while I was finishing up my bowl of cereal. He poured himself a cup of coffee, gave us each a kiss, and grabbed his paper.

"Good morning, what are the two of you up to?" he asked.

"Oh, not too much. I'm about to head upstairs to do school and mom is currently writing her acceptance speech for Meanest Mom in the World," I said.

"You know, if this were any other family, I might actually probe more into that statement, but knowing you all as I do, I think I'll just quietly sip my coffee and read my paper," said dad.

Mom walked over to where dad and I were sitting just as Aunt Christine sluggishly entered into the kitchen in search of coffee.

"Oh, good, you're just in time," said mom.

"In time for what," yawned Aunt Christine.

"In time to hear my speech," replied mom. "According to Beau I'm the meanest mom in the world because I'm making him read poetry, so I thought I'd prepare a little speech and then post it onto Facebook for everyone to enjoy."

"Oh, this ought to be good," she drawled.

Mom cleared her throat, picked up a bottle of dish soap, and held it as if it were an Oscar. "Wow, thank you, this is so completely unexpected!" She set the dish soap down and smiled humbly as if she were to address a room full of strangers. "I would first like to thank the child that nominated me, because without you, this award would not even be possible. If it weren't for your poor attitude, inability to do as I say, constant insubordination, and complete inconsideration, I would not be standing here today. I would also like to take a moment to acknowledge each and every nominee in this category. You know who you are, and just knowing that I am not alone, that there are others out there willing to fight the good fight and refuse to raise obnoxious little jerks, gives me the motivation to continue to be the meanest mom I can possibly be." She looked lovingly over at dad, "And to my husband, Greg, what can I say? You are the yin to my yang. You are always there to lend a kind word whenever I feel I'm in over my head. Anytime I start to think about throwing in the towel, you are the first person to stand up and say, 'Don't let those little bastards win!' You. Complete. Me." She scanned the room as if an entire audience were watching her, "Lastly, I would like to thank the beverage that keeps me sane, wine, because without you, I might very well be residing in a jail cell." She lifted up the dish soap in celebration, "Thank you. Thank you all so much!"

"Wow, I can see you've had entirely too much time on your hands this morning," snarked Aunt Christine.

"Well, to be fair, I've been mentally preparing this for years, so it really didn't take very long." She closed the box of cereal sitting on the counter and placed it back in the pantry. "I also figured that today would be as good a day as any to claim my crown, so I just thought I'd go ahead and formalize it a bit."

Well, I for one, thought it was great, honey," said dad. He unfolded his paper and began reading the front page, "And, of course, the mere fact that you had the forethought to even mention my name before thanking the wine was both moving and humbling, so thank you."

'Admittedly it was a toss-up, but it just seemed to flow better, you know?" she winked.

"I love you too, sweet cheeks," he said, blowing her a kiss.

Mom turned to me, "Addie, honey, I'd like to head over the library in about an hour, will that work with your school schedule?"

"Yeah, that should be fine," I said. "I've already been able to get a good bit done this morning and can always finish the rest once we get back."

I got up, rinsed out my bowl, and went upstairs to study while dad headed to his home office for work. Mom and Aunt Christine were drinking coffee and chatting about their plans for the day when Grandma Helen swept breezily through the back door.

"Girls, I'm so glad you're here, I just came up with the most brilliant idea for the Angel Tree." She hastily made her way to the kitchen and helped herself to a cup coffee, "I'm practically bursting at the seams, I'm so excited!" She opened the refrigerator and immediately looked over at mom, "Olivia, honey, where's the peppermint mocha creamer I asked you to get?"

"I haven't had time to go to the grocery store yet, so you're just going to have to make do with what's in there, sorry," said mom.

"Ugh, hazelnut, how depressing," she pouted.

"Well, good morning to you too, mother," said Aunt Christine sarcastically.

"Oh, don't think of me as unkind, darlings, it's just that it's Christmas, and I'm really wanting my coffee to taste like it, that's all."

"'I'll see what I can do," said mom.

"Ooh and get some of that frosted sugar cookie creamer too, will you?" she asked. I just love Christmas, it's always so festive and fun!"

"I'm putting it on my list right now," said mom jotting the item onto her notepad. "So, tell us, what's this great idea you've come up with?"

"Oh, yes the idea," she said excitedly. "Okay, so I was putting on my make-up this morning, and as I started to blend in my cocoa-colored bronzer, I began thinking about all of the poor little Hispanic boys and girls on my Angel Tree list, and how rather than just dropping off all the gifts unceremoniously in some dilapidated hovel, we should instead invite all the families to the theater for a Christmas celebration with food, drink, and perhaps even a surprise visit from Santa, himself!"

"Oh, mom, I think the families would love that!" said Aunt Christine.

"Chrissy's right, they would," agreed mom. She reached over and gave Grandma Helen's hand a light squeeze, "You know, mom, I have to say it's really nice to see you getting into the Christmas spirit like this."

"What's that, dear?" she asked distractedly, "Oh, yes, Christmas spirit…anyway, I was thinking to make it even more fun, I'd dress up as Mrs. Claus and then serenade Santa up on the stage with my Santa Baby number." She clapped her hands giddily, "Then we invite all of the local news stations and really give them a special Christmas story to blast across the airwaves!"

"With you as the headliner, I take it?" asked mom.

"Well, it is my idea, dear, so it only makes sense that I would." she said.

"Have you run any of this by Joan or Tobias?" asked Aunt Christine.

"Or any the board members, for that matter?" added mom.

"No, not yet, but I'm certain they'll see the benefit of it all." She sipped her coffee contemplatively, "I mean, if you look at it pragmatically, you'll see that everyone benefits. The theater is getting free advertising, the poor people are getting presents, and I'm getting to perform, so you see it's really a win, win, win situation for everyone!"

Just then Beau walked in to ask mom when she was planning on leaving to go to the library. He was wearing bright yellow Sponge Bob pajama bottoms, a red and green tie-dye t-shirt, and filthy beat-up sneakers he absolutely refuses to throw away.

Mom took one look at him in that get up and said, "I'm sorry, son, but there's no way you're going to be wearing that out in public today."

"What? Why not?" he asked.

"Because you look ridiculous, not to mention you're completely mismatched." She motioned toward the stairs, "You have a closet full of nice clothes, so please go back upstairs and choose something a little more appropriate."

"Well, what about when I wear jeans and a green shirt?" he asked earnestly. "That doesn't match, and yet you're fine with that."

"I'm not even going to dignify that with a response," she said.

"And you've let me wear this outfit over to Tyler's house a million times," he pointed out.

"Yes, well, Tyler lives next door, and his mother allows him to use his clothes as a napkin, so it's never really been much of an issue before." She folded her arms in front of her, "But today we are going over to your grandparents house, the library, and to the dollar store, so you need to make yourself look presentable, at least."

"Well, if we're shopping at the dollar store, I'll fit right in," he stated proudly.

"Listen, you are not about to make us look destitute simply because you can't put an outfit together, so please, for the love of everything that is Holy, go and change your clothes," she said.

"Ugh, fine, but I want to go on record as stating that I make this outfit look good!" he barked as he stomped back up the stairs.

"Duly noted, son," she called out after him.

"Oh, what an enjoyable morning," trilled Grandma Helen. "I absolutely adore watching you in your natural element, Olivia, you're such a good mother."

"Yes, well, I highly doubt Beau would agree with that statement right now, but thank you," said mom. "Anyway, back to the matter at hand, I think the idea of having a Christmas party in honor of the Angel Tree is a wonderful idea, mom."

"It is, isn't it?" she said. "Okay, well, I'm off to the theater to share my brilliant idea with everyone else." She helped herself to another cup of coffee and merrily made her way to the back door, pausing briefly before saying, "Oh, and do be a dear, Olivia, and send my love to George and Carol. In fact, you may even want to let them know about the Angel Tree Christmas party. I'm sure Carol would love the opportunity to make some of her little pecan thingies to share with everyone."

"Pecan pie bars? You hate those," said mom.

"Yes, darling, but she doesn't know that," she winked.

"I tell you, that woman is a walking dichotomy," said Aunt Christine, watching her strut confidently out the door.

"Well, that's certainly one way to describe her," agreed mom.

An hour later, we were just about ready to leave when Beau remembered that he needed to bring the books he had previously borrowed from the library. He quickly ran upstairs and then came back down holding two rather thick books in his hands. Mom hadn't been with us the last time we went to the library, so she was surprised at the sheer volume of each paperback he was holding. You see, the thing about Beau is that he loves the idea of reading but hates the actual act of doing so. He also loves going to the library in search of books he knows full well will never be opened in his presence, yet that never seems to deter him from bringing many of them home. Mom usually lets him check out whichever books he chooses in the hopes that he will one day surprise her and actually read one, but the likelihood of something like that happening would be akin to Grandma Helen becoming an ambassador for the UN's refugee agency. It's just never going to happen.

"In the future, Beau, would you please refrain from bringing books the size of *War and Peace* home from the library, let alone two?" asked mom. "There is absolutely no way you'll ever be able to finish a book that size in a two-week period."

"Yes, I can," he said.

"Really?" asked mom. "I haven't seen you pick up either one of those books the entire time they've been here."

"Hey, I read one page," he said indignantly.

"Wow, one page, huh?" Mom grabbed her keys and headed toward the back door, "Well, you may want to see if you can extend your loan about 15 years because at the rate you're going, that's when you'll finish."

"I personally think I'll be able to do it in ten but go ahead and be negative if you want." He followed her out the door, "What is *War and Peace* anyway?"

"A very long, tedious, and incredibly overrated work by a man named Leo Tolstoy," she said, locking the door.

"Oh, okay, cool, maybe I can bring that one home too," he said excitedly.

***

We had no sooner entered the library when Beau tried to sneak off toward the fiction aisle, in search of Leo Tolstoy and his 1,225-page novel. Mom immediately reeled him back in and then guided him in the opposite direction saying, "Oh, no you don't, mister. We need to head over to the science section and find some books for your science paper, remember?"

"Ugh, fine," Beau acquiesced.

We both followed mom to the back of the library where the science books were shelved. As she and Beau were making their way down the aisle, I took a seat at a nearby desk and pulled out my laptop. I could overhear their conversation perfectly, as did everyone else in the library, because neither one of them has the capability of holding a quiet conversation, especially whenever they discuss anything school related.

"Okay, since you've decided to write your research paper on the planet Earth, you're going to need to find two different sources that can help you do that." Mom gestured over to where I was sitting, "I'll be with your sister if you need me."

Just as she turned to leave, he said, "Oh, I think these two are exactly what I'm looking for!" He lifted up two books and smiled widely, "*Earth* and *Earth*."

"Are you serious?" she asked.

"What, I found two books about Earth, I thought that's what you wanted me to do," he said.

"Don't you think you should, I don't know, look inside them to see that they actually have the relevant information you need?" she asked.

"They're both about Earth, so I'm pretty sure that's the information I'm going to need," he said. "Besides, the cover on both of these books look so amazing!"

"It's never wise to judge a book solely by its cover, Beau," she said.

"Why wouldn't I judge a book by its cover? That's the first thing I see, and if it's not interesting to me, why would I want to take it home?" he asked.

"You know what, never mind." She took a deep breath and tried a different tack. "Listen, we're here to find books that will help you write a paper about planet Earth, so the first thing you're going to need to do is figure out what it is exactly that you're wanting to research about the planet Earth. Once you have figured that out, you're going to need to find two separate sources that can help you understand those ideas better, and in order to do that, you're going to need to verify that the books you choose can, in fact, provide the information you seek. So, you see, it's not necessarily going to be that simple."

"Well, I'm pretty sure that *Earth* and *Earth* are both going to help me do that," he said.

She stared incredulously at him for a few seconds before finally conceding, "Okay, fine, *Earth* and *Earth* it is, then."

"Great!" he exclaimed. "Now, let's go and find *War and Peace!*"

CHAPTER TEN

After leaving the library, we got in the car and headed over to Nana and Pop's house. I was in the front seat scrolling through my phone and Beau was in the back looking over his recently acquired literary masterpiece when Carly Simon's *You're So Vain* started to play on mom's SiriusXM 70's radio station. She immediately turned up the volume and began singing along unabashedly with Carly as she intimately described the narcissistic tendencies of a self-loving, self-absorbed past lover who wore an apricot scarf and a hat strategically dipped below his eye. It was the sort of song my mother loved to sing, not because it was a great way to torture my brother and me (that was just an added bonus), but because she truly revered the singers and songwriters of the sixties and seventies and often considered them to be true poetic geniuses.

"You're so vain! You probably think this song is about you. Don't you? Don't you?" she sang out proudly. She looked over at me, "Come on, Addie, sing with me!"

I'm good, mom, thanks," I said.

"Oh, you're no fun," she poked at me playfully. "I happen to know that you love this song because I heard you singing it in the shower just the other night."

"That's what you were singing?" asked Beau incredulously. "Wow, you sounded nothing like this."

"Be nice, Beau," said mom. "Not everyone has the gift of song."

"Yeah, well, tell that to all my brain cells that committed suicide that night. It was awful, mom." he grumbled.

"I'm surprised you even had any brain cells to lose in the first place," I retorted sourly.

Before Beau could respond in kind, mom began singing loudly again.

"Well you're where you should be all the time
And when you're not, you're with some underworld spy
Or the wife of a close friend, wife of a close friend, and..."

She continued along with the final chorus and then turned down the volume just as the song began to fade out, "I tell you, that woman really knew how to write a song. She was always so emotive and honest with her lyrics; it's truly a shame that most artists today can't write a song even close to that anymore."

"If you say so," mumbled Beau.

"I take it you don't like Carly Simon?" asked mom.

"She sings well enough, but she doesn't make a lot of sense," he said.

"Oh, and how is that?" she asked.

"Well, first of all, what guy is willingly going to wear an apricot scarf? That in and of itself was a giant red flag for me." He caught her eye in the review mirror as she continued to drive, "And second of all, that song has everything to do about him, so what is he supposed to think? I mean she just keeps going on and on about all the things he's done and then tells him that he's probably going to think the song is about him; well, duh, it is about him!" He picked up his book and pretended to read the back cover, "Seriously, if she's just going to hurl insults at him all day, the least she can do is admit that she wrote the song about him."

I looked over at mom, "I hate to say it, but he actually makes a valid a point."

"That he does," nodded mom in agreement. "You know, Beau, I don't think I've really ever given it much thought, but I think you may be right about that."

"I know," he smiled confidently.

"Yes, well, even a blind squirrel can find a nut every once in a while, I suppose," I said.

"Shut up, Addie," snarled Beau.

"You know what I think we need?" interjected mom. "I think we need some good old fashioned Christmas music to get us into the Christmas spirit." She turned the station over to the Holiday Traditions channel just as the final notes of Bing Crosby's *White Christmas* had finished playing.

"I don't know about the two of you, but I'm really looking forward to decorating the tree on Friday; I hate seeing it so barren right now." She glanced over at each of us, "Thank you, by the way, for putting it up for me."

"Yeah, no problem," I smiled.

"I don't know why your saying anything, Addie, all you did was spread out a few branches," snarked Beau. "Ezra and I did most of the work while you sat on your phone the entire time."

"I'm sorry, but Dusty called, and I had to take it," I replied coolly.

"Tell me, do you also salivate every time he rings a bell too?" he asked.

"Shut up you little jerk!" I snapped.

Before Beau had a chance to yell back, mom quickly interjected once again, "Speaking of Dusty, is he still planning on coming over to help us with the decorations?"

I sneered back at Beau before answering her question, "Yes, he is."

I took mom's cell phone charger and plugged it into my phone, "I also made sure to warn him about grandma and all of her eccentric tendencies, too."

"Good, I definitely think that was a wise and prudent decision," she said.

"Well, he keeps saying that he's really excited to meet her and the rest of the family, so I'm just hoping it goes smoothly, you know?" I said.

"That guy won't last the night," snickered Beau.

"That's enough, Beau," warned mom.

He balled up his fists and pretended to cry like a baby, "RIP, Dusty, it was fun while it lasted."

"Shut up, Beau!" I yelled.

"Stop telling me to shut up, you shut up!" he retaliated.

"I hate you! You're such a troll." I said.

"I hate you more!" he spat.

As we drove through the gates that led into my grandparent's neighborhood, the happy and cheerful voices that were currently caroling *Joy to the World* on the radio were now completely drowned out by Beau and me as we continued with our loud, incessant, and often creative insult exchange. No longer able to tolerate another minute of our feud, mom pulled over to the side of the road, slammed on the brakes, and unleashed her inner demon. "Both of you shut up!" she screamed. "I am not in the mood for this today and I really don't feel like having a mental breakdown in front of your grandparent's house, so please, for the love of God, stop your bickering!" She looked at each of us in turn, "I am so sick and tired of the way you two speak to one another and I want it to stop, do you understand me? It's Christmas, for God's sake! We're supposed to be happy and joyful, not angry and spiteful."

We both stared silently at her as beads of perspiration started forming on her forehead and upper lip. She blew out an exasperated breath and immediately started fanning herself with her hands, "Oh, great, now I get to deal with this."

"Uh, why are you all pink and wet?" asked Beau, his lip curled.

"I'm having a hot flash, Beau," said mom irritably. She turned on the air conditioning to full blast, "And you and your sister are not helping the situation."

"I'm sorry, mom," I said penitently, "I know that can't be very comfortable."

"It's fine, honey, it'll pass." She quickly turned all the air vents in her direction, "I just need the two of you to get along, please."

"What's a hot flash?" asked Beau.

"It's just the body's way of reacting to menopause, that's all," she said.

"What's menopause?" he continued.

"Well, it's a natural biological process that affects women of a certain age. Often times the estrogen levels in the bodies of older women tend to-"

"You know what, I don't need to know, I'm good," he cut her off.

"Beau, it's nothing bad, it's just a hormonal imbalance, that's all," she clarified.

"Yeah, um, that's gross," he said.

"How is that gross?" I asked, bewildered.

"I don't want to know about mom and all of her feminine problems, Addie," he said disgustedly.

"Well, you don't need to be a jerk about it," I said.

"You know what, it's fine," said mom. "He's not ready to learn, and that's perfectly understandable." She smiled over at me, "It's fine, honey, let it go."

A few minutes later, we were pulling into the circular driveway that ran across the front of Nana and Pop's house, a beautiful red brick colonial they purchased shortly after moving here from Mississippi. Upon exiting the car, we could hear the faint and distant hum of a chainsaw running in the back of the property over by where Pop's work shed stood.

"Oh, cool, I think Pop's is cutting up logs, can I go and help him?" asked Beau excitedly.

"That's fine, but please be careful, Beau, I really don't need you losing a limb before Christmas," said mom.

As Pop's was stacking the recently cut wood into a pile, he looked up just in time to see Beau running toward him. He immediately stopped what he was doing and with a wide grin, waved happily over to both mom and me before opening his arms wide for Beau to run into. He then reached into his bag and grabbed some ear protection for Beau before carefully walking him through all the steps of chainsaw etiquette. Knowing that Beau would be blissfully occupied with Pop's and his yard work for a little while, mom and I took this as our cue to go inside and find Nana.

***

Nana absolutely loves Christmas. She loves the decorations, the baking, the music, the gatherings, the merriment…everything, and her home reflects that adoration in intricate detail. Each room looks as though it were plucked from the pages of a *Southern Living* magazine, complete with Magnolia Leaf garland, rustic farmhouse Christmas wreathes, and ornately decorated table centerpieces. It is the epitome of southern holiday charm and evokes a feeling of unexplainable peace and comfort. The simmering of apple cider, cinnamon, cloves, and orange peel on the stovetop helped to bring it all together by making the entire house not only smell like Christmas but feel like it too.

As mom and I made our way into the living room, we immediately caught sight of an immensely tall and oversized Leyland Cypress standing in the corner. It housed a multitude of decorations in various shades of green, gold, and red, all of which sparkled amongst the white twinkling lights threading their way intricately throughout its branches. There were also dozens of small handmade red bows tied to each limb for an additional enhancement of color. The entire room felt cozy and warm, and very reminiscent of Nana.

"Where does that woman even find the energy to do this year after year?" asked mom.

She bent down to pick up one of the gifts strategically placed under the tree. It was wrapped in plain brown kraft paper with three ornate pleated sections on top. Inside one of the folds were trimmings made from fresh cut pine, red berries, and a tiny decorative cotton branch. She pulled out the small name tag nestled inside one of the other folds, "And when exactly did she start wrapping like Martha Stewart?"

I looked down at the rest of the gifts lying under the tree, each one uniquely wrapped in matching color schemes, "I think ever since she discovered YouTube." I looked back up at mom, "Maybe you could watch a few videos and learn to wrap like that too."

She looked at me as if I had grown a third eye, "I'm sorry, but have you ever watched either one of your brothers open a gift? They don't just unwrap it; they violently assault it." She set the gift back down under the tree, "Taking the time to do something like that would just be an exercise in futility."

As we stood admiring the room around us, we could hear the faint sound of Christmas music playing from the back of the house. Realizing it was coming from the sunroom, we started to head that way in search of Nana. We found her standing in the middle of the room, surrounded by five large easels, looking as though she were deep in thought, contemplating something important. She immediately perked up the minute she saw us walking through the door.

"Hey, y'all!" she said in her sweet southern Mississippi drawl. "I was wondering when y'all we're gonna get here."

"Hi Nana," I said, giving her a big hug.

"Sorry, we had to make a quick stop at the library," said mom. She surveyed the arc of easels scattered around the room, "So, what have you got going on here?"

"Oh, my painting class is going to be starting in about thirty minutes," she said, looking at her watch. "I'm trying to get set up before everyone gets here."

"Painting class?" asked mom.

"Yes, I started teaching one a few months ago." She placed a small jar of paint brushes on the tables that separated the easels, "Every three months, the five of us vote on a painting that we want to paint, often times it's themed, and then we work on them together here in my sunroom." She lifted up an unfinished painting, "We're currently finishing up this little Christmas village, isn't it adorable?"

"Yes, very cute," agreed mom.

"Ooh, I love all the red cardinals sitting in the trees," I said.

"That was my idea," she winked. "A little added addition to make the painting even more festive and colorful."

"Oh, I see, so it's really more like a painting club, rather than a class?" asked mom.

"No, it's a class," corrected Nana.

Mom walked over to one of the easels and looked at the painting that was resting on its base. It was only partially painted and still covered with a bunch of small black numbers.

"Wait, so you're actually giving a painting class using paint by numbers?" She looked perplexed, "I'm not trying to be rude, Carol, but how exactly does something like that even work? A paint by numbers is pretty straight forward, you just look at the number, match it to the color, and paint, right?"

"Well, it's not always that easy," she smiled sweetly.

"It's not?" asked mom.

"Oh, heavens no!" She beckoned for mom and me to follow her over to one of the paintings, "Take the snow in this painting, for instance. Rather than douse the number with paint, which often leaves the canvas looking bumpy, I have learned to use a white paint marker to hide the number, which inevitably ends up saving me both time and paint." She referenced a different quadrant within the same painting, "I have also taught my students to paint lighter areas before darker ones because it helps to create a good finish, and to use toothpicks to fill in teeny tiny areas like the ones you see right here."

Nana walked over to her own workspace and put on her artist smock, "I've also been teaching them how to avoid smudging, how to blend, and how to enhance their paintings so that they look more realistic, so you see, there is plenty to be learned in this class." She tied the strings hanging from the back of her smock, "And the paint by number canvas' tend to give us a good base to work with, so it's just easier to use those."

"Wow, I had no idea this was even a thing," said mom. "It's honestly quite impressive."

"Oh, well, it's really nothing more than me just sharing some of the tricks and techniques I've learned over the years," dismissed Nana. "Honestly, it's really more about the comradery of the group for me. You know, just a smattering of old retirees with plenty of time on their hands looking for something fun to do."

"That's great, Nana," I said. "I'm so happy you've found some friends that you can paint with now."

"It definitely looks as though you've found your niche, Carol," said mom. "I'm happy for you too."

"Aww, thank you, darlin," she drawled. She put her hands on her hips and then exhaled a deep breath, "Well, I suppose I had better get you those cookie tins before George sees them and throws them away."

We followed her into the kitchen where a large box sat on the counter, filled to the brim with cookie tins of various shapes and sizes, and completely covered in Sharpie markings that read, "Not Trash!" and "Do not touch!" There was also a note attached that said, "This is for Olivia, so keep your mitts off of it, you old codger!"

"I tell you, that man is unsufferable," she said stopping in front of the box. "He knows full well that I don't want to throw certain things away, but the minute my back is turned, it somehow miraculously makes its way into the dumpster."

Mom peeked inside the box, "Thank you so much for saving all of these for me, I really appreciate it. I have a lot of baking to do this weekend, and these will be perfect to give to friends and neighbors."

"Well, anytime I can prove to George that not everything is trash, and that some people may actually benefit from my propensity to save, is more than enough thanks for me, honey," she smirked.

Mom lifted up the box and carefully made her way over to the kitchen door that led out into the side yard, "Addie, honey, can you please open the door and then go ahead and get your brother?"

"Yes, ma'am," I said, quickly hugging Nana before opening the door.

Mom was just about to walk through the door when Nana stopped her by saying, "Oh, and Olivia, please tell your mother that I would be more than happy to make some of those pecan pie bars for the Angel Tree party."

Mom paused in the doorway, "Oh, she called you already?"

"Yes, it was earlier this morning, but I just haven't had a chance to get back to her yet." She smiled excitedly and crossed her arms in front of her, "You know, I had absolutely no idea she loved them so much. She just went on and on about how great they were, and how I absolutely had to make a large batch so that everyone at the party could try them."

"Oh, yes, she really does love them," lied mom, unsure of what else to say.

Nana leaned in close and spoke softly, "Well, don't tell her this, because I want it to be a surprise, but I'm planning on making her a few dozen as well."

"Oh, Carol, you don't need to do that," said mom hastily. "You're making them for the party, and that is more than enough, believe me."

"Oh, nonsense!" she said, waving her off. "Your mother is an absolute saint for orchestrating this whole celebration, so it's really the very least I can do." She looked down at her watch and then back up at mom, "Okay, well, I need to go and get ready for class. Make sure to send my love to everyone, and remember, don't tell Helen about my special little surprise!"

CHAPTER ELEVEN

After leaving Nana and Pop's house, mom needed to make a quick stop at the dollar store to see if they carried a special nail file that her friend, Marissa, had been telling her about. As we pulled into the parking lot, we were immediately greeted by several advertisements depicting a small group of Dollar Tree employees, smiling happily in their bright green polo shirts, promoting job opportunities, hourly pay, and benefits. There was even a $500 signing bonus for anyone willing to work full-time, making it quite clear that the Dollar Tree, was not only in dire need of employees, but more than willing to pay handsomely for them as well.

As we exited the car, a giant box filled with oversized Christmas Candy yard décor immediately caught Beau's attention. He ran out and made a beeline for one of the enormous red and white candy canes protruding from the box and lifted it up excitedly.

"Mom, we seriously have to get some of these for our yard!" he exclaimed.

"Maybe," she said noncommittally.

"Okay, you and I both know that's the same thing as saying 'no' in mom speak." He lifted another one with his other hand, "Come on, mom, these are so cool!"

"That's not entirely true, Beau," she said. "Besides, you know the outdoor decorations are your father's domain, not mine, so I really have to defer you over to him anyway."

"Well, can you at least put in a good word for me?" he asked. "Because I think these would look totally awesome lined up on our walkway."

"Yeah, I think I can do that," she winked.

We entered the store and immediately made our way over to the counter where a young woman with spikey blue hair and multiple facial

70

piercings was manning a register. Her eyes, lips, and nails were all painted black, but the most disturbing ornamentation was definitely the three-inch black widow tattoo that rested across her throat. The large silver hoop piercing her septum and the massive wad of gum residing in her mouth made her look every bit like a goth cow casually chewing its cud, or at least according to Beau, it did. She seemed to be completely engrossed in the pages of a tattoo magazine and reluctantly dragged her attention over to us only after my mother cleared her throat, alerting her to our unwanted presence.

Knowing Beau's propensity for unfiltered speech, mom discreetly placed her arm around his shoulders, giving her hand direct access to his mouth, as she took a moment to read the girl's nametag.

"Hello, Draven, I'm hoping that you might be able to help me with something," she said.

Draven, who looked to be incredibly slovenly, heaved a heavy sigh and returned her attention back to her magazine as if we weren't even there.

Gritting her teeth, mom continued, "A friend of ours found a certain nail file here not too long ago. It's about the size of a regular nail file but has four sides to it. Do you happen to remember seeing anything like that?"

"Not sure," said Draven, shrugging her shoulders.

Doing her best to tamper down the desire to yank the young woman's hoop ring from her nose, mom feigned a smile, "I see, well, my friend said that she found a stack of them up by the cash register, but it doesn't look as though you have any. Do you happen to know if you have any stocked in the back or perhaps maybe they were moved somewhere else in the store?"

"Uh-uh," she shook her head.

"'Uh-uh', you don't know or 'uh-uh' you don't have any stored in the back?" asked mom.

"Umm, I don't know, I guess both," she said, chomping her gum.

"You know what, Draven, never mind, I'll just look elsewhere," said mom irritably.

As mom and I turned away to make our grand exit, Beau continued to linger in front of the counter perusing the various candy offerings. He looked up at the laggard standing in front of him and casually said, "Well, I can certainly see why the Dollar Tree has five giant signs looking for help outside." He picked up a Milky Way and tossed a dollar bill onto the counter, "And considering the fact that a trained monkey could more than do your job, Draven, you might really want to reevaluate how you treat your customers, especially those that have the capability of making your life miserable. You're just lucky that it's Christmas time and my mother is feeling charitable, because otherwise you'd be wishing you'd been a little more accommodating and a little less impertinent." He then took his candy and strutted right out the door with the biggest smirk across his face.

Mom and I immediately followed, and before either one of us had a chance to say anything, he quickly stated, 'Don't worry mom, I'm not going to eat this now, I just thought making a purchase and tossing a bill on the counter would add a little more drama to my statement, you know?"

"Beau, you definitely outdid yourself in there, and have more than earned your right to eat that candy bar right now." She tussled his hair lovingly, "I appreciate your support, honey."

"Really?" he asked.

"Yes, really," she smiled.

"Oh, my gosh, and I didn't even have an ulterior motive, or anything. I was just trying to prove a point." He tore open the candy bar excitedly, "Wow, that felt good! I don't know where half of those words even came from, but I was actually able to use one of my vocabulary words from last week."

"Oh, yeah, and which one was that?" asked mom.

"Impertinent," he said. "You made me use it in five different sentences last week, and I think it finally stuck!" He took another bite of the candy, "And you're right, mom, being well-spoken totally has its advantages, so I'm definitely going to start paying better attention to you every time you yell at me."

"Um, thank you, I think," said mom, a little taken aback.

We climbed into the car, buckled our seatbelts, and were just about to back out of the parking space when mom's cell phone began to ring.

Looking down at the screen, she could see that it was Grandma Helen, so she immediately pressed the connect button on her steering wheel, "Hi, mom, just so you know, you're on speaker and I have the kids in the car."

"Are you warning me or preparing them, dear?" said Grandma Helen, her voice enveloping us in the small space.

"Neither, mother. I just thought you'd like to know in case you were planning on mentioning anything about their Christmas gifts, that's all," said mom.

"Oh, I'm not calling about any of that," she said dismissively. "With all that's on my plate right now, I honestly haven't even had time to think about the children, let alone shop for them."

"Gee, thanks grandma, we're all looking forward to spending the holidays with you too," said Beau sarcastically.

Mom looked behind her seat at Beau and shook her head disapprovingly, warning him not to go any further.

"Oh, now darling, you know that your grandfather and I are planning on getting you something for Christmas, so there's absolutely no need for you to pout," she admonished. "Besides, there are still plenty of shopping days left, so just give me a list and we'll see what we can do."

"Sure thing, grandma, I just hope there's enough room on your plate for me and my list," snarked Beau.

Mom immediately whipped around in her seat and silently gave Beau the death glare while Beau shrugged his shoulders innocently as if to say, "What are you getting so mad about?"

As the two of them continued to gesticulate back and forth, I quickly chimed in, creating a diversion.

"Hi grandma!" I said, perhaps a little too excitedly.

"Adelaide, darling, where is your mother? Have we lost her?"

"Oh, um…" I said.

"Olivia are you still there?" she asked.

"Yes, mom, I'm here," said mom breathlessly.

"What's going on, is everything alright?"

"Everything's fine, mom, I just had to fix something in the back of the car, that's all," said mom, throwing Beau a reprimanding glare.

"I see," she said. "Well, listen, darling, I really need you to do me a favor; where are you, exactly?"

"We're just about to head home from the Dollar Tree, why, what do you need me to do?" asked mom.

"Oh, dear god, is that anything like that godawful Dollar General they insist on placing outside every neighborhood in the south? I mean,

73

honestly, nobody needs that many dollar stores in one place, and the drab yellow color makes it look just like Waffle House, and you know how I feel about that place. I mean, surely, they could at least make it look a little more inviting and little less repellent."

"I know you're not a fan, mother, you make it perfectly clear every time we drive by either one of them," said mom. "Anyway, what is it you need me to do?"

"Oh, yes, I need you to swing by the Salvation Army for me, dear. Apparently, there are a few more Angels that are still in need of sponsoring, and I need you to pick them up so that we can add them to our Walmart shopping list."

"Yeah, I can do that, no problem," said mom.

"Wonderful, darling," she trilled. "Oh, and just so you know, they're planning on closing early today for some kind of inventory counting, or something, so just knock on the door and they'll let you in."

"Okay, well, we're headed that way now,' said mom.

"Thank you, darling," she said cheerfully, disconnecting the call.

Mom turned the key in the ignition, "Well, she was at least able to refer to Walmart without curling her lip like she normally does, so I suppose that's progress."

"Wait, Grandma's actually going to step foot in a Walmart? Oh my gosh, that's classic!" laughed Beau.

"She's doing it for charity, Beau, so please keep the sarcasm to a minimum," said mom.

He shoved the last of the Milky Way into his mouth and snickered, "I'll be sure to offer up a prayer; those poor Walmart employees are going to need it."

***

The Salvation Army was located only a few miles away from the Dollar Tree, so it really didn't take long to get there, but Grandma Helen was right, they had definitely closed up early for the day. We knocked on the front door, and the manager, Doris, a sweet older woman with kind eyes and warm smile, graciously ushered us in. She explained that she was in the process of helping another person but would be with us shortly, so rather than sit idly on an old worn-out sofa, we opted to wander the store for a bit. As we did, we could overhear Doris speaking Spanish to a young woman, while the young woman's daughter, quietly played with a three-story dollhouse in the corner of the store.

While Doris continued to help the woman fill out paperwork, mom and I decided to head over to the book section. Beau, who had ditched us the moment we walked in the door, was currently perusing the music offerings in the back of the store. When it comes to music, Beau is an old soul. He loves anything from the 70' and 80's, and has even been known to like a few obscure bands from the 60's. He prefers vinyl to anything modern and tends to turn his nose up at any type of repress because they don't have all the crackling sounds like old-time records do. This love and appreciation for both records and retro music came about after spending a few weeks with dad's younger brother, Uncle Eric, a couple of summers ago. He's definitely the music guru of the family and has really taken Beau under his wing, teaching him everything he knows about music and records. He currently lives in Plano, Texas with his wife, Jennifer, and their twin daughters, Rose and Lily. Unfortunately, the distance makes it difficult to see each other as often as we would like, but we still do our best to keep in touch either through weekly phone calls or summer vacations.

"Oh, my gosh, mom, they have so many records!" said Beau excitedly. "They even have a *Hall & Oates* one; can I please get it?"

"I think they're already closed for the day, honey, so I don't think you can make any purchases," answered mom. "Besides, Christmas is coming, and you never know what you might be getting."

"Ugh, fine," he capitulated. "Can I at least come back tomorrow and get it?"

"We'll see," said mom.

Before Beau even had the chance to argue, Doris was motioning for us to join her over by the register. She had a large manilla envelope in her hand and was just about to give it to mom when she overheard the young Hispanic woman telling her daughter that they needed to leave the dollhouse where it was, but that maybe in a week or two, they could come back for a visit. Doing her best to choke away tears, the little girl took a deep ragged breath, nodded her head somberly, and obediently took hold of her mother's hand.

"Um, would you excuse me for just a moment?" asked Doris.

"Yes, of course," said mom.

Immediately taking her leave, Doris walked over to the young woman, gesturing toward the dollhouse as she did. Even though we weren't entirely sure of what was being said, it was evident by the tears in the mother's eyes that Doris had just offered to gift the dollhouse to them. The young woman kept shaking her head, refusing the kind offer, but Doris just continued to smile and encourage the young woman to accept the gift for what it was, a Christmas offering. After a few minutes of gentle persuasion, the young woman finally agreed, and the transaction was finished.

As we watched the two of them walk the little girl back over to the dollhouse, mom and I dabbed at the corner of our eyes. We had just witnessed a Christmas miracle, and it had literally moved both of us to tears. Beau, who had been privy to the same miracle, immediately looked over at us and stated plainly, "Okay, if she's getting a dollhouse out of this whole thing, I'm pretty sure I can hold out for the *Hall & Oates* record."

CHAPTER TWELVE

Later that afternoon, mom and Beau were sitting at the kitchen table hunched over a giant map of the United States, while I completed the geometry test I wasn't able to get to this morning. I was really looking forward to getting this test done, too, because once I did, I would be out for Christmas break and not have to worry about school until January. Beau still had two more days left, but he was banking on mom letting him out early; she was both exhausted and running on fumes, so the odds of it happening were definitely in his favor.

"Okay, last one, show me where Massachusetts is and tell me the capital," said mom.

"Oh, it's right here and the capital is Columbus," said Beau pointing to the upper right corner of the map.

"The location is correct, but the capital is actually Boston," she said.

"Well, at least I was close," he shrugged.

"And in what way is Columbus even remotely similar to Boston?" she asked.

"Oh, you know, just switch a few letters around and you'll get the gist of what I'm saying," he answered pragmatically.

"Honey, I don't think anyone's ever going to get the gist of what you're saying," she said, rolling up the map. "It doesn't make any sense."

"Well, that's unfortunate," he quipped.

Mom put the map away and then handed Beau his book, "Okay, time to read."

"What?" he exclaimed. "It's already 5:00 and way past the time we normally end school."

"I understand why you might be upset, but the visit to your grandparent's house, along with the other stops, has put us little bit behind," she said.

"A little bit?" he shrieked. "Mom, I really think you need to reassess your concept of time because there was nothing little about it."

"Go," she pointed upstairs.

"But reading is so boring," he stomped his foot petulantly. "I mean, all you ever do is just read words lined up on a page."

"Gee, Beau, your ability to conspicuously point out the obvious in such an eloquent and ardent manner truly astounds me once again," said mom.

"I don't even know what some of those words mean!" he bellowed.

"That's exactly my point," she said. "Reading will help you expand your vocabulary."

"Ugh, why can't I just go and play like other kids?" he pouted.

"Because I love you," she said.

"That doesn't even make any sense!" he cried out.

She walked over to him and lovingly cupped his face, "I tell you what, read your three chapters without complaint and we'll consider this your last day before Christmas break. How does that sound?"

"Okay, wait a minute, am I being filmed?" he asked, looking around the room suspiciously. "Like, is this some kind of deranged version of *Impractical Jokers*, homeschool edition, or something?"

"No, you're not being filmed," she laughed.

"So this isn't a prank?" he looked at her askance.

"It's not a prank, Beau, I promise." She stacked the books scattered across the kitchen table, "I just think we're all in need of a break, I know I am."

"Yes, thanks, mom!" he said, hugging her gratefully.

"You're welcome, now go and read," she said.

Beau strutted confidently in my direction, mouthing the words, "Told ya" right before bounding happily up the stairs to read his three chapters. Rolling my eyes inwardly, I picked up my completed test and took it over to mom, "You know you just gave him exactly what he wanted, right?" I said.

"No, honey, I gave him exactly what I wanted, a nice long break." She pulled the teacher's manual out from under the pile of books and took a seat, "Once I finish grading this test, I am completely finished with the semester and won't have to worry about anything school related until next month." She smiled up at me and pointed to one of the chairs, "Have a seat, let's see how you did."

I took the seat across from her and sat nervously as she graded my test, hoping that the final grade would reflect all of my hard work over these last few months. Mom tends to struggle with geometry, so for added practice, I took it upon myself to find outside sources to help me with the things that she doesn't quite understand. It's been a tremendous help, and although I feel fairly confident in my mathematical ability, I am still incredibly anxious to see my final grade.

"Addie, you did it!" she exclaimed, lifting my paper so that I could see my grade. "This just secured your 4.0 for the semester!" She jumped out of her chair and hugged me tightly, "Oh, honey, I'm so proud of you!"

"Thanks, mom," I said, hugging her back. "I really appreciate your help this semester."

"Honey, you did all the work, not me," she laughed. She placed the test in her file folder and started putting the stack of books away, "You know, if you keep getting grades like that, you won't even need to worry about earning a soccer scholarship because your grades will earn one for you." She looked over at me, "Speaking of which, have you given any more thought to the colleges we've been visiting lately?"

"I have, but nothing's really stood out to me yet," I said.

"Well, just be sure to look closely at the school itself, and not just the soccer program," she said pointedly. "If you get injured, you're going to want to make sure you're at a school that makes you both happy and provides a good solid education. You don't want to wind up some place that makes you feel miserable and stuck."

"I know, and that's what I'm trying to do," I said.

Mom headed into the kitchen to start prepping for dinner, "So, do you have any desire to stay close to home?" she asked, maybe a little too hopefully.

I smiled, knowing full well she didn't want me to stray too far and was praying I that would choose a school that would keep me close by. "Most likely, yes," I said. "I think I've also decided that I'm more interested in attending a smaller D2 college, rather than a larger D1 school, so that should help narrow down some of the options as well."

"Oh, and what made you decide that?" she asked.

"I love playing soccer, but I don't want it to overrun my life. I have friends that are playing D1 right now and they're miserable, and even though I know that a D2 school will have its own challenges, I won't have to be tied to soccer morning, noon, and night. I want to enjoy my college years, not regret them."

"Well, I think you're making a very wise decision." She stepped out from the pantry and set a few things on the counter. "Besides, we still have plenty of time to think about all of this. You're only a junior, so there's really no need to make any decisions right away."

We were in the middle of discussing the pros and cons of D1 and D2 colleges when Grandma Helen walked breezily through the back door, "Olivia, darling, do you happen to have that list of Angels from the Salvation Army, I asked you to pick up earlier?"

"Uh, yes, I think I set them right next to my purse," said mom, nodding toward the far end of the counter.

"Thank you, dear." She grabbed the manilla envelope sitting beside mom's purse and then looked lovingly over at me, "And how is my beautiful granddaughter doing today?"

"I'm good, grandma," I smiled.

"Have you been out with that Dusty boy, lately?" she asked, her brows raised.

"Uh, no, we've both been too busy with school and other obligations," I said.

"Oh, well, I'm certainly looking forward to getting to know him," she cooed. "Tell me, does he paint well?"

"Uh, I don't know, why do you ask?" I looked at her suspiciously.

"Well, I was just thinking that he may want to help the theater paint props from time-to -time, that's all. You know, put in a little work and maybe make a good impression." She opened the envelope, slid out the sheet of paper, and scanned the list of names, "I am, after all, the matron of the family, so it would definitely do him well to get on my good side," she winked.

I stared silently over at mom, willing her to intervene on Dusty's behalf.

"Stop it, mother," said mom. "Dusty's not going to want to paint your props, and don't you dare ask him to do it either!"

"Oh, don't get so uptight, Olivia, I was simply asking a question." She slid the paper back into the envelope, "So, what time are you wanting to leave tomorrow, dear?"

"Well, considering we're on Christmas break now, I'm fairly free, so I suppose whenever you'd like," said mom.

"Oh, that's wonderful, darling!" trilled Grandma Helen. "Now you can help me plan the Christmas Extravaganza at the theater."

"Extravaganza?" repeated mom. "I thought this was just supposed to be a small gathering for all the Angel Tree recipients, not a full-blown party," said mom.

"Darling, there are going to be television camera's present, so no, a simple gathering it most definitely is not," she snickered.

"Spectacle sounds more like it," mumbled mom irritably.

"I heard that, dear," said Grandma Helen, giving her the side-eye. "Anyway, why don't we plan for ten tomorrow morning, that way we can grab a nice lunch once we're done and decompress from the day."

"Decompress? Since when does shopping ever cause you any stress?" asked mom. "It's your favorite thing to do other than to perform and promote yourself."

"Since I'm being forced to shop in that godawful store against my will, Olivia." She paused momentarily, squinting over at the can sitting on the counter next to mom, "What exactly is a Manwich, dear?" she asked, slowly enunciating the two syllables.

"It's a sloppy Joe, mother," said mom. "And before you even say anything, which I know you inevitably will, the kids love them and I'm too tired to do anything else."

"I see," she said, curling her lip. She watched mom empty the contents of the can into the pan of cooked meat, "Well, I suppose there's no accounting for taste." She then quickly turned on her heel, strutted out the back door, and called out, "Enjoy your slop!"

***

"Ooh, Manwich, my favorite!" said dad excitedly, as he took a seat at the table. "These look delicious, honey, thank you."

"Well, I'm not entirely sure that my mother would agree with that assessment, but you're welcome," said mom.

Ezra came downstairs and immediately took a seat next to me. He looked down at his plate and said, "So, mom, are the green beans just for décor or are you actually expecting us to eat them?"

"Ezra, you're twenty years old, don't you think it's time to add at least a few healthy options to your diet?" she responded.

"I'm actually good with the way things are, but thanks anyway," he retorted.

"Seriously, Ezra, you really need to take better care of yourself now that you're getting older," said mom. "You're not always going to be able to eat what you want, when you want, and it will eventually catch up with you, so you may want to start taking precautions now."

"Which is exactly what prompted me to buy a bottle of Flintstone's vitamins the other day," he said, unfolding his napkin and placing it in his lap, "Those babies are going to be a gamechanger, mom, I just know it!" he winked.

"Well, I suppose that's progress," she said, reaching for the salt and pepper. "Oh, I meant to ask earlier, how did it go with your last midterm? Are you officially done for the semester?"

"It went well, and yes, I'm done," he said. "I should be getting my grade later tonight."

"What's an intern?" asked Beau.

"Midterm, honey, not intern." clarified mom.

"An intern is someone Bill Clinton uses, a midterm is an exam that you take during the middle of a school year," said dad, casually taking a bite out of his sandwich.

Mom practically choked on her food, "Greg!"

"Well, it's the truth," he shrugged.

As the rest of us were laughing hysterically at dad's impromptu vocabulary lesson, Beau was struggling mightily with his sandwich. "Aww, man, this is too hard to eat."

"How have you managed to completely disintegrate your sandwich in such a short period of time?" asked mom.

"I don't know, it just keeps falling apart on me," he said, working to piece it back together.

"All is not lost, son, just put the sandwich down and use your fork," said dad.

"A fork?" He lifted it as if it were a foreign object, "What am I supposed to do with a fork?"

"You can't possibly be serious right now," said dad.

"It's completely falling apart, dad, how is a fork going to make it any better?" He looked down at the mess on his plate, "Seriously, what do you expect me to do with it?"

"Oh, I don't know, maybe stab yourself in the eye and then use your ear to eat your sandwich," said dad sarcastically. "What do you think, son?"

"Just eat it with a fork like you would a casserole," interjected mom calmly.

"Oh, I get it now, duh!" he laughed. "I guess it's kind of like when I have to eat my pizza with a fork because it's too hot and everything just slides off onto the plate." He happily scooped the disintegrated sandwich onto his fork and took a bite, "This is so much easier, thanks dad."

"Hey, has anyone seen my Martha Stewart cookbook?" asked mom. "There's a recipe in there I'm going to need for Christmas dinner, and I can't find it anywhere."

"I think I remember you telling me that you were going to put some of your cookbooks in the guest bedroom closet, so you may want to check there," I said.

"Oh, that's right, I did, thank you honey!" she smiled. "I'll have to look after dinner."

"Speaking of Martha Stewart, did any of you know that she was on the cover of *Sports Illustrated*'s swimsuit magazine this year?" asked Ezra.

"I did, yes," said mom. "She looked great too."

"I don't know, it's just kind of strange to see an older woman like that posing in a swimsuit, you know?" he said.

"Well, I just hope that I can look that good when I'm 81," said mom.

"God, I hope you do too," joked dad.

"Hey, wait a minute, is that the same woman that makes cakes on TV and then eats them?" asked Beau.

"She actually does a lot more than that, Beau," said mom. "She was one of the first people to make home and hospitality a marketable business and is now considered to be one of the richest women in the world, with multiple thriving companies under her name and brand."

"Well, Tyler's mom said that she went to jail for two years because she didn't pay her taxes, so it doesn't sound like she's a very good person," he said.

"Yes, that is bad, but people often make mistakes. We just have to hope that they learn from them," said mom.

Dad wiped his mouth with his napkin and set it atop his plate, "You know, you should probably inform Tyler's mom that many of our members of Congress do the exact same thing, yet nothing ever happens to them because, unlike the rest of us, they are apparently above the law and above reproach."

"Um, yeah, I don't think I can remember all of that," said Beau.

"That's okay," winked dad, "I'll write it down for you."

CHAPTER THIRTEEN

"Oh, for Christ's sake, mother, you're Christmas shopping at Walmart, not parachuting into Normandy," said mom, rolling her eyes. "Let's just get out of the car, already."

"That's easy for you to say, dear, you're amongst your people," said Grandma Helen, gesturing at the disheveled mother wrestling her toddler into the car seat next to us. "I, on the other hand, am a foreigner traversing an adventitious land, so you're just going to have to be patient with me while I do my best to mentally prepare."

The three of us had been sitting in the car for ten minutes while Grandma Helen practiced her diaphragmatic breathing, a ritual she says she performs nightly before ever stepping foot on stage. This particular breathing technique is quite popular amongst the acting community and is often used to lower heart rate and blood pressure in those suffering from chronic pain, mental distress, nervousness, and apparently, the occasional Walmart Supercenter visit.

"Patient? Mom, we've been nothing but patient. We've sat here patiently listening to you breathe like a dog in heat for the last ten minutes," snarked mom. "And now the windows are almost completely fogged up."

"You know, a little appreciation for what I'm about to-" she cut herself off midsentence and then said, "What is that?"

"What is what, mother?" asked mom.

"That dirty white heap on the ground over there," she said, pointing to the recently vacated parking space across from us. "What is it, exactly?"

Mom looked over to where she was pointing, "I think it's a diaper."

"Oh, dear god, I don't think I can do this," she shuddered involuntarily. "You two go on without me, I'll stay here."

"Save the theatrics for the stage, mother. We've been sitting in this car long enough, so let's just get out and go do what we came here to do," said mom irritably.

Grandma Helen dropped down the visor in the passenger's seat and carefully checked her lipstick, "Yes, well, if we happen to come across more dirty diapers strewn about the parking lot, we're going to have to navigate it like a mine field." She flipped the visor back into place and grabbed her purse, "I mean, honestly, how rude can some people be?" She grabbed hold of the door handle and heaved a heavy sigh, "I'm going to be needing a stiff drink after this, Olivia." She pulled on the handle and then looked back over her shoulder, "Do you hear me? Stiff."

We exited the car and mom immediately pulled me in close as we followed behind Grandma Helen, "Don't let her out of your sight for one minute, and if you happen to foresee any snide verbal combat about to take place, do whatever you must to shut her up."

"What do you want me to do, tackle her to the ground?" I snickered.

"I'd prefer you be a tad bit more discreet, but whatever it takes, I suppose," said mom.

I looked at her in complete shock, "I'm not going to do that!"

"Okay, fine," she rolled her eyes. "Look, you just never know what's going to fly out of that woman's mouth, so just be prepared to initiate some form of damage control, okay?"

"Okay," I nodded.

As we neared the front entrance, we came upon a pleasant looking young woman standing next to a collection bin, joyfully ringing a bell. She wore a large red apron with The Salvation Army logo emblazoned across the front and a personalized Santa hat that read, "Twila" on its brim. She was smiling and waving at everyone, but her warm greeting seemed to go unnoticed as each person hastily rushed by in search of the bright blue shopping carts lined up just inside the door. Unwilling to allow their indifference to affect her, she continued ringing her bell as if she hadn't a care in the world. She had just bid farewell to a departing shopper when she caught sight of Grandma Helen walking toward the sliding glass door.

"Merry Christmas, Helen!" she waved excitedly.

"Is it, Twila?" mumbled Grandma Helen, continuing to make her way past the young woman.

"Mother don't be rude," hissed mom. "The least you can do is return her greeting."

Grandma Helen paused momentarily to look pointedly at mom, "Talking to that girl is like opening up Pandora's Box, Olivia. Trust me, it's best if we just keep walking."

"You can't just go around treating people like that, mother," said mom accusingly. "The girl obviously knows you, so at the very least, you should stop and say hello."

Grandma Helen pursed her lips and raised a brow, "Okay, fine, you win, but just remember, I did try to warn you." She turned and slowly sauntered back over to Twila, lightly tapping her on the shoulder, "Merry Christmas, dear, are you enjoying your little bell?" she asked.

"Oh, hi, Helen," said Twila excitedly. "I thought I heard you say something when you passed by, but since you just kept walking, I wasn't so sure."

"Yes, well, I was deep in thought," said Grandma Helen. "Twila, darling, I don't believe you've met my daughter, Olivia and my granddaughter, Adelaide. They were both gracious enough to accompany me today on my little shopping trip."

"Oh, hello," said Twila, "It's nice to meet you."

"Twila has recently started working at the theater, you see, and has been instrumental in helping Ben, our stage manager, with varying backstage tasks," said Grandma Helen.

"Well, I actually started a few months ago and have just been having the time of my life helping with all the costume and prop changes. I've been going to the theater since I was a little girl, so when the opportunity presented itself to volunteer backstage, I jumped on it. My aunt works in the ticket office, she's the one that actually told me about the opening and helped me get the position. I just love watching everyone perform, too. I mean, who would have ever thought our small town would have so much talent? Not me, that's for sure!"

"Yes, well-" said Grandma Helen.

"I'm just kidding!" she guffawed. "You know, I never would have pegged you for a Walmart shopper, Helen. Are you here to get some of your Christmas shopping done or just jotting down some ideas for your list? Oh, wait, I know, you're probably shopping for the Angel Tree gifts!

Joan was telling me all about that the other day, and I just think it's so wonderful that the two of you are planning a special party for all those kids. I even hear that a certain special someone from the North Pole is expected to make a visit. I mean, it just wouldn't be a Christmas party without an appearance from the big man himself, am I right?"

"Yes, well, we had better-" said Grandma Helen.

"So that must make you two Helen's special little helper elves," interrupted Twila again. "Although I must say, I think you both might be a wee bit too tall to be Christmas elves," she giggled at her own joke. "My mom always tells me that I would make the perfect elf because I'm so small. I'm only 5'2, so she definitely has a point, but I really wish I was taller. Shopping for clothes can be such a challenge. I mean, even the petite section can be too big for me, you know?"

"Twila, we really must-" said Grandma Helen.

"Honestly, though," she continued, "I think what you and Joan are doing is great for the community. Oh, and just so you know, there are a ton of great sales going on right now, so you should probably be able to get a really good bang for your buck, if you know what I mean. Hey, that reminds me-"

"Goodbye, Twila," said Grandma Helen, effectively dismissing her with the flick of the wrist, "I'm done pretending to be nice."

"Oh, okay, well, be sure to stop by on your way out," she called after us. "That way we can pick up where we left off!"

Mom and I immediately took our leave and chased after Grandma Helen, wanting to get as far away from Twila and her endless spiral of verbal regurgitation as quickly as possible. "Oh, my god, that girl is like a hyped up chihuahua on speed," said mom. "I don't even think she took a breath the entire time we stood there."

"I told you we should've just kept walking, dear, but no, little miss holier than thou just had to stop by and say hi," said Grandma Helen, carelessly flinging her purse into a shopping cart. She took a few tentative steps, looked around, and sighed, "Ugh, I see poor people."

"Stop it mother," said mom.

Ignoring mom's admonition, she looked down at the handle of her cart. "Olivia, why is everything so sticky?"

"It probably just needs to be wiped down, that's all," said mom.

"Wiped down?" she curled her lip. Letting go of the handle, she immediately looked down at her hands and gasped in horror at the tiny red broken pieces of candy clinging to her palms and fingers.

"What in the actual-"

Before Grandma Helen could even finish the sentence with her favorite expletive, mom immediately jumped into action and threw a handful of antibacterial wipes at her. "Here, just use these and then go wash your hands."

"I…I…I," she stuttered, staring repulsively down at her hands.

"Look at me mother," said mom, trying to be the calm in the storm. "It's candy not blood, so there's no need to act as though you're the sole survivor of a mass casualty." She pointed over to the front of the store, "Addie will take you to the restroom so that you can wash your hands and I'll get you another cart, completely devoid of anything unpleasant."

"This place is hell on Earth, Olivia," she spat. "I hate it here!" She turned toward me, her voice wobbling a bit, "Addie, do be a dear and get my purse, I think we're going to be needing to decontaminate that as well."

Once Grandma Helen had washed her hands and taken a few moments to collect herself, she and I made our way back over to mom, who had since plastered a warm smile on her face and was currently presenting the new shopping cart like Vanna White would a recently deciphered phrase on the wall.

Unimpressed, Grandma Helen grabbed the shopping cart, pulled out her list, and said, "I propose that we start in the toy department and then go from there." She then raised her chin defiantly, "And if either one of you so much as mentions this little mishap to anyone, I will personally see to it that neither one of you make it into my will."

She turned abruptly, making her way past an older gentleman wearing a blue Walmart vest, joyfully welcoming shoppers. "Happy Holidays!" he said enthusiastically.

"Not here, it's not," she shot back.

Mom and I quickly grabbed two shopping carts and immediately set out after her. You wouldn't think a person of Grandma Helen's age and stature would be able to get away from someone that fast, but the woman has a set of wheels on her that could rival any short distance runner, so the fact that she was able to leave the two of us wandering aimlessly in her wake was really no surprise at all. Once we were finally able to catch up with her, though, we saw that she was already hard at work, filling her cart with various Barbie dolls and Disney Princesses.

"Wow, Grandma, that was fast," I said.

"Yes, well, I'm not one to dawdle, dear." She marked a large X across her list and walked over to the next aisle. "Oh, good, here we go, cars." She hastily grabbed several different cars from the shelves and haphazardly tossed them into mom's buggy. She then marked another large X below the first one and said, "Okay, sports equipment, now, where would I find that?"

"Mom are you even paying any attention to the specificity of the list?" asked mom, picking up a Mermaid Barbie randomly laying atop the pile in Grandma Helen's shopping cart. "I mean, is there a child that is actually requesting a mermaid, or did you just throw it in the cart with everything else?"

"What exactly is your point, Olivia?" sighed Grandma Helen irritably.

"My point is that we may need to slow down and make sure that we're actually giving these kids what they want," she answered.

"It's a Barbie, it's free, and it's feminine, what more could a poor little girl want?" she asked.

"Oh, I don't know, something with legs, perhaps?" replied mom.

"Ugh, fine!" She hastily tore the list and handed the bottom half over to mom, "Here, you go and shop for the boys and Adelaide can monitor me as I shop for the girls. Will that make you happy, dear?"

"Yes, I believe that it will work just fine, thank you," smirked mom.

The two of us watched mom leave with her half of the list and then headed back over to the doll aisle. "Alright, Addie, tell me, what does the first child on the list want?"

Reading the torn piece of paper in my hand, I said, "Um, the first little girl is asking for a baby that cries and pees."

"A baby that cries and pees?" she repeated. "Why in the world would anyone want to willingly succumb themselves to something so abhorrent?"

"She's a little girl, grandma, she's probably just wanting to mimic her mom in some way," I said. "It's what little girls do."

She plucked the list from my hands and slowly read over it. "It says that this child has five siblings under the age of six. Don't you think buying her a doll that cries and pees would be an act of redundancy?"

Before I even had a chance to answer, mom walked purposefully around the corner, grabbed the doll in question and threw it into Grandma Helen's basket, "Try not to be such a bitch, mother."

CHAPTER FOURTEEN

"Please tell me we're near the end of all this tedious procurement, dear," said Grandma Helen, carelessly tossing a pair of children's *Sesame Street* tennis shoes into her cart. "I'm honestly quite tired of shopping for other people."

"Stop whining like a four-year-old, mother," said mom. "You've certainly never had any issues spending five hours in Neiman Marcus, so I'm pretty sure you have the stamina to spend at least two hours here."

"Yes, but Neiman's is a much more pleasant shopping experience, darling." She picked up another pair of shoes and tossed them into the cart, "There's even a quaint little café overlooking the entire first floor that serves the most divine Shrimp Louie salad and cheese biscuits." She looked imploringly over at mom, "Can't we just leave here and go there, dear?"

"No," said mom.

"Well, can we at least go and get something to drink?" she pressed. "My throat is parched and I need something strong to make me forget about this insufferable place."

"Look, we're going to be meeting Christine for lunch after this, and in the meantime, I'm sure Addie will be more than happy to go and get you a bottle of water," said mom, nodding animatedly in my direction. "But until we do, you're just going to have to suck it up like the rest of us."

"I don't want water, I want vodka!" she stomped her foot petulantly.

"And we will get you some, mother, I promise," appeased mom. "Listen, we really don't have that much left to do, so-" she stopped midsentence, her eyes growing wide in panic.

"What?" asked Grandma Helen, matching her panic. "Is it my hair? Is it my make-up? What is it?" She urgently reached into her purse, pulled out a compact, and carefully studied her reflection, "Well, nothing seems to be amiss; I seem to look just as fabulous as I did when I stepped out of the car." She snapped the compact shut and looked disapprovingly over at mom, "You know, you really mustn't scare me like that, Olivia. I thought I was having a make-up malfunction for god's sake."

"Uh, sorry," said mom distractedly, slowly making her way back into the shoe aisle. "I was just, um…thinking that, um…that these children might benefit from more than one pair of shoes, that's all." She intently studied the rows of shoes in front of her, "You know, maybe one pair with laces and one with Velcro straps?"

Knowing my mother to be a terrible liar, Grandma Helen immediately caught on to her charade and slowly turned around to see for herself what the source of her discomfort was. Standing in the aisle directly across from us, stood Lacey Simmons, our ebullient and over-the-top neighbor who has the uncanny ability to grate on mom's nerves like no one else. You see, Lacey is a braggart, so when she's not giving a personal account to everyone about how amazing her life is, she's shamelessly flaunting it across every form of social media imaginable. The woman overshares every single aspect of her life, including the self-imposed prodigious lives of her four perfect (no, they aren't) children. Whether it be an unplanned Starbucks run, midmorning workout, or Department of Motor Vehicles visit, you had better believe Lacey was going to let everyone and their mother know about it.

"Isn't that Lacey Simmons over there?" asked Grandma Helen.

"No, I don't believe so," said mom, suddenly taking immense interest in the pair of boys *Batman* slippers she was holding. "Tell me, do you think any of the boys on our list would like a pair of these?"

"You're avoiding her, aren't you, dear?" asked Grandma Helen, raising her brow knowingly.

"Don't be ridiculous, mother," she snickered. "I'm a grown adult, I don't do things like that."

"Is that so?" she smirked. "Well, if that's the case, then you won't mind if Adelaide and I meander on over there to say hello, now, will you?"

"Don't you dare!" hissed mom.

"Oh, stop acting like a disgruntled pelican, Olivia, and pull yourself together," said Grandma Helen.

"Keep your voice down, mother!" said mom, crouching covertly in the aisle, "And stop quoting Moira Rose, this isn't *Schitt's Creek*."

"Well, it'd be a lot more fun if it was," mumbled Grandma Helen.

"Why are you hiding from her, anyway, mom?" I asked. "Did she do something to upset you?"

"Not particularly, no," she said. "I just don't have it in me today to stand there for thirty minutes, nodding politely as she drones on and on about her perfect children and her perfect life." She peeked out from behind the large red and white Rollback price sign concealing her position, "I have to either be in the right mood or three sheets to the wind to deal with that woman, and since I'm neither, this is where we're finding ourselves."

"Tell me, dear, why exactly are we having to go out of our way to avoid your source of vexation, but mine was practically shown a welcome mat?" asked Grandma Helen.

"I apologize, mother, but to be fair, you could have at least forewarned us that Twila was a compulsively hyperverbal maniac. Lacey may be self-aggrandizing and vainglorious, but at least I can get a word in edgewise." She looked over at me, "That means pompous and boastful, by the way."

"Yes, mother, I know," I rolled my eyes.

"Okay, well, the next time I go out of my way to ignore someone, I fully expect the two of you to follow along," said Grandma Helen, pointing her finger at mom and me.

The three of us watched patiently as Lacey leisurely walked up and down the aisles, pausing here and there to add things to her cart. She was just about out of eyesight when she stopped abruptly to take a picture in front of an endcap filled with diapers and baby wipes.

"May I ask a dumb question?" asked Grandma Helen.

"Better than anyone I know," quipped mom.

"Aren't we witty?" she smirked. "You know, for someone working so hard to stay under the radar, you certainly are brave to joke with me like that, dear." She returned her gaze back over to Lacey, "I'm curious, though, what in the world makes a person want to take a selfie with a bunch of diapers?"

"Who knows?" shrugged mom. "That woman is the queen of documenting the mundane, so it's most likely going to end up on Facebook under a caption that reads something like, 'My future grandbabies will be pooping rainbows, what will yours be doing?'"

"Well, that's imbecilic," said Grandma Helen.

"Yes, well, most of her social media posts usually are," said mom.

We waited a few more minutes for Lacy to finish her improvisatory photo shoot before quickly making our way back up to the front of the store. After scrutinizing and carefully examining each of the twelve lines that led up to the highly coveted registers, Grandma Helen finally settled on one, blowing out an irritated breath as she did.

"You know, it's bad enough that we have to stand here and be herded like cattle, but now I'm going to have to suffer through The Carpenters *Merry Christmas, Darling*, while I do it?" She crossed her arms fractiously in front of her, "You know, I've honestly never even understood their appeal. They've always sounded so blah and bland, not to mention monotonous and repetitive; and don't even get me started on their stage presence and costumes."

For those of you that don't know, The Carpenters are a popular brother and sister duo from the seventies who's distinctive soft musical style and harmonizing helped to create multiple top-ten hits during their often strained and complex 14-year partnership. Karen Carpenter, who many categorize as one of the top female vocalists of all time, and who's voice, Sir Paul McCartney once called "melodic, tuneful, and distinctive," is also the same voice that drives Grandma Helen to inwardly convulse anytime she hears it. You see, in her distorted mind, it is literally the equivalent of fingernails down a chalkboard, so the fact that she can recognize it playing in the background, despite the flurry of activity and craziness around us, is really not surprising.

"Don't start, mother, please," mom rolled her eyes.

"I'm simply making an observation, dear, that's all," she clarified, "There's no need for eye-rolling."

Fortunately, our line moved relatively quickly so we were all somewhat surprised to find ourselves walking up to a vacant register as promptly as we did. The entire area was brimming with holiday shoppers, screaming children, and completely devoid of any of the joy one might normally associate with the month of December.

"What is this?" asked Grandma Helen, standing awkwardly in front of a large cumbersome looking machine. "Where are all the little blue helper people?"

"This is self-checkout, mother, so we're going to have to do it ourselves," said mom.

"I'm sorry, what did you just say?" asked Grandma Helen.

"It's self-checkout." She pointed over to the long line of carts on our right, "And unless, you'd rather get back in line over there and wait another 30 minutes for someone else to do it, I suggest you start scanning."

"You mean to tell me that after spending two long hours in this godforsaken place, I'm now expected to scan and bag everything myself?" she shrieked.

"I guess that's the price you pay when you don't want to pay a lot for things," shrugged mom apathetically.

"You're enjoying this, aren't you, dear?" she raised her brow.

"Maybe a little bit," winked mom.

"Fine, I can do this." Resolving herself to her fate, Grandma Helen squared her shoulders and turned intentionally toward the odd-looking machine positioned behind her. "And how exactly does one operate this monstrosity?"

"You just scan the item and place it in a bag, grandma," I said. "It's really easy."

Taking a deep breath, she grabbed the first item from her cart and ran it across the scanner. "It's not doing anything." She continued swiping it over and over like a madwoman, "Why isn't it doing anything?"

"You need to scan the barcode, mother," said mom, stifling a laugh.

"And what's that?" she asked.

"I picked up one of the toy trucks from my own cart and turned it over to show her the barcode, "Somewhere on the packaging you'll see a bunch of lines and numbers in a square box, like this one, and that's what you're going to want to swipe across the scanner."

"Oh, dear god, this is going to take hours." She handed mom the Malibu Barbie she was holding, "Here, you do it."

"Ten bucks, pay up," smiled mom smugly. She held out her hand expectantly to me, "That was entirely too easy."

"Ugh, fine," I said, reluctantly reaching for my wallet. "You win."

"Am I missing something?" asked Grandma Helen.

"I bet Addie that you wouldn't get past the first item in your cart before handing it off to me." She happily took the $10 bill I slapped into her palm, "She apparently doesn't know you as well as I do."

"Yes, well, I'm so glad that my predictability could earn you a profit, dear," said Grandma Helen. "Now you can put that money to good use by buying me a very cold and very dirty vodka martini."

Mom and I had finally finished scanning and bagging everything and were just about to pay when someone called out loudly, "Hey, how much longer are the three of you gonna be? You're taking forever, and some of us have lives, you know."

Grandma Helen, completely unaffected by the dig, glanced briefly over her shoulder to see a rather large and rotund woman staring menacingly back at her. She was wearing a pair of nude-colored leggings that left very little to the imagination and a snug t-shirt that read, "Donuts Make Me Happy."

"Just let it go, mother," murmured mom, under her breath.

Grandma Helen, never one to back down from a fight, haughtily looked the woman up and down, grabbed her receipt, and then turned to casually confront her, "Yes, well, judging by the look of you, I can't imagine it's much of one, dear."

She then turned on her heel and walked confidently out the door, careful to avoid Twila and her constant, frenetic bell ringing.

CHAPTER FIFTEEN

"Bless you, my child, you always were my favorite," said Grandma Helen, sliding into the booth next to Aunt Christine. She quickly drained the dirty martini sitting on the table in front of her and sighed contentedly, "Oh, dear God, I needed that; thank you, my darling."

"Actually, Ollie's the one that told me to have it ready for you, so you may want to redirect your adoration over to her," said Aunt Christine. "Where is she, anyway?"

"Dad called on our way in, so she's outside talking with him," I said. "She did say to order her a glass of chardonnay, though."

"You know, dear, you can always go back to being my favorite daughter if you walk up to the bar and get me another one of these," she smiled, wiggling her martini glass.

"Here you are, my darling," cooed a regal looking gentleman, as he set down another martini in front of her, "and don't worry, I'll be sure to keep them coming."

"Justin, darling!" exclaimed Grandma Helen, "You read my mind, thank you." She gratefully took a sip and then casually placed her hand atop his, "I just had the most dreadful experience of my life shopping at Walmart, so yes, I will most definitely need you to keep them coming."

"Oh, you poor thing, I can't even begin to imagine how awful that must have been for you," he soothed. "That place just sucks the joy right out of shopping, if you ask me."

"It was horrible, absolutely horrible," she shuddered. "I just want to put it all behind me."

"Jesus, mother, it's not like you single-handedly took out the leader of a drug cartel, you simply went shopping for a few hours," muttered Aunt Christine.

Giving her the evil side-eye, she said, "Justin, do be a dear and bring out a few extra bleu cheese stuffed olives with the next one, will you? You know how much I love them."

"Of course, darling, anything you need," he said, taking his leave.

"Sorry, Greg called and I needed to take it," said mom, sitting down in the booth. She nodded over at the two martini glasses sitting in front of Grandma Helen, "I see you've been busy, mother."

"Yes, well, I need to forget all about this day, and vodka can help me do that," she raised her glass high in the air, "Cheers, my darlings!"

"Was it really that bad?" asked Aunt Christine.

"No," said mom.

"Yes," answered Grandma Helen. "It was execrable."

Aunt Christine looked over at me, "And what do you think, Addie? Should we start setting up weekly shock therapy appointments to purge it all from her brain?"

"Um, I think I'm going to stay out of this one," I said wisely.

"It really wasn't that bad," dismissed mom. "We had a few hiccups here and there, but nothing that I would categorize as 'execrable.'"

"Oh, and then there was that abhorrent woman standing in line behind us that taunted me," added Grandma Helen. "That woman was the epitome of all things Walmart."

"The one you verbally slapped?" I laughed. "Yeah, I don't think she was expecting you to say anything."

"Yes, well, thank God it didn't turn into an episode of *Maury Povich*, with her pouncing on you at the checkout counter," interjected mom. "I'm fairly certain that video would have made the rounds on TikTok and every other social media outlet had it escalated."

"So, what exactly did you say to this woman?" asked Aunt Christine.

"I simply pointed out that her appearance wasn't doing her any favors, and that the speed in which I conduct my checkout is not to be blamed for her monotonous and unremarkable life," answered Grandma Helen nonchalantly. "Well, maybe not in so many words, but you get the gist of what I said."

"Ouch," she said, under her breath. "That wasn't a very Christian thing to do, mom; especially during Christmas."

"I never said I was a saint, dear," said Grandma Helen.

"Yes, mother, but you may want to consider toning it down some, that's all," said mom. "People are crazy enough as it is, and you never know how someone might react to being humiliated like that, especially in public."

She sat quietly for a moment, contemplatively sipping her martini, "I suppose you have a point, dear." She toyed with the olives in her glass, "Although, I'm not going to lie, it did feel good to put that woman in her place." She picked up her menu and casually read over it, "You know, sometimes I think life would just be easier if I could follow Jesus and slap people too."

"Eloquent, as always, mother," said Aunt Christine.

"So, what sounds good to everyone?" I asked, picking up my menu.

"Umm, where's my wine?" asked mom.

"Oh, I think we forgot to order it, dear," said Grandma Helen distractedly, as she perused the menu.

"You mean to tell me that you've already had two drinks and mine hasn't even been ordered yet?" She mumbled irritably under her breath, "You people are unbelievable."

"We're unbelievable?" repeated Aunt Christine. "Tell me, dear sister, why, exactly, is the wine advent calendar empty?"

"They were mini bottles, what did you expect?" asked mom.

"Well, I certainly I didn't expect them to be gone so quickly, that's for sure," she said. "We have almost two weeks until Christmas, Ollie, and Greg didn't even bring it home until a few days ago, so the fact that it was completely empty was a just a bit surprising, that's all."

"Was it really, dear?" interjected Grandma Helen doubtfully.

"Well, what I'm supposed to do with a six-ounce bottle of wine, exactly?" she picked up her menu and pretended to read, "I mean it took three day's worth to fill up one wine glass for god's sake, so yes, the advent calendar was done for relatively quickly." She glanced up and rolled her eyes, "Sorry."

As if on cue, Justin walked up to the table and set a large glass of chardonnay down in front of mom, "I believe this is for you, darling."

"Thank you, Justin," she smiled.

"Of, course," he said, with a tilt of his head.

"Wait a minute, if they didn't order it, how did you know to bring me one?" she asked.

"I texted him, dear," said Grandma Helen.

"Yes, Helen and I exchanged numbers a few months ago so that she could easily notify me of her need for refills." he explained.

"And it's been a match made in Heaven, hasn't it, darling?" she cooed.

"It's definitely been something," he smiled tightly, pulling out his notepad and pen. "Now, what can I get you lovely ladies?"

We ordered lunch and were in the process of discussing tomorrow's tree decorating party, when Beau's smiling face lit up mom's phone.

"Hi, honey," she answered.

"Hey mom, you know, I was thinking, is it alright if I get one of my gifts tonight since you let my sister have her phone early?" he asked.

"No."

"Tomorrow night?"

"No."

"Why not?" he whined. "You let Addie have her big gift early, so it's only fair that I get one of mine early too."

"And what makes so sure that you have more than one gift," she smirked.

"Wow, that was dark, mom," he said.

"Look, your sister needed a new phone, and that's why she received it early," explained mom. "There was no hidden agenda or desire to make you feel less important or less loved. It was simply done out of necessity, that's all."

"Oh, I see, so, my sister gets a new phone, and what do I get, I get an exercise in patience," he snarked. "Thanks so much for your generous and benevolent gift."

"Goodbye, Beau, I love you," she said, effectively ending the conversation. "Nice use of vocabulary, by the way."

"Yeah, I love you too," he responded. "But just know, I'm going to remember this when we're deciding what to do with you and dad in 40 years."

"I'll be sure to take that under advisement." She ended the call and reached for her wine, "That child truly tries my patience."

"Yes, well, all children have their moments, dear," said Grandma Helen.

"You know, I just don't ever remember being that dramatic over trivial things," she said.

"Surely you're joking, right?" asked Aunt Christine.

"What?" asked mom. "When was I ever dramatic?"

"*Project X*," they answered simultaneously.

"What is *Project X*?" I asked.

"Oh, just some movie about monkeys your mother made us all go to," said Grandma Helen flippantly. "It was supposed to be funny but ended up being quite distressing."

"Okay, to be fair, that movie came out right after *Ferris Bueller's Day Off*, and they promoted it like it was comedy, so how was I supposed to know it was going to end like that?" asked mom.

Noticing the look of confusion on my face, Aunt Christine kindly elaborated, "It was an 80's movie about chimpanzees, not monkeys, that just so happened to throw your mother in to a frenetically uncontrollable emotional tailspin that just about got us banned from the theater."

"It was supposed to be a comedy!" reiterated mom.

"Your mom's right, it was definitely advertised as a comedy, and since it was released right after Matthew Broderick had just finished *Ferris Bueller's Day Off*, we had no reason to think otherwise. Of course, there were a few comedic parts here and there, but it wasn't until the end of the movie, that it became apparent that the chimpanzees were being tested on, and not always pleasantly, if you catch my drift." She took a deep breath, "So, Ollie, being the animal lover she is, had a complete mental breakdown during the scene and not only hyperventilated, but wailed so loudly, that mom and I had no choice but to move quietly to other seats."

"Nine rows," clarified mom. "You people moved nine rows away from me."

"And yet, we could still hear your howling, dear," said Grandma Helen, sipping her martini. "I remember I couldn't get out of that theater fast enough that day; I practically sprinted to the car."

"You've always been such a pillar of support, mother," drolled mom.

We were all still laughing at mom and her PETA breakdown when Justin came by with our entrees. He carefully set everything down and then came back with another martini for Grandma Helen, who was currently in the process of finishing her second one.

"Thank you, darling," she said. "I don't believe I'll be needing another one, but do stay alert, just in case."

"Of course, my dear," he said.

"Are you feeling better now, mother?" asked Aunt Christine. "Cleansed, perhaps?"

"Yes, dear, I believe I am," she smiled. She lifted up her martini glass, "And now, all of those hellacious flashbacks I was having are becoming nothing more than a faint memory, thanks to the lovely makers of Grey Goose."

"Well, thank God for that," she snorted. "Life threatening situations can certainly take a toll on a person's mental well-being, so I'm glad you're able to find some solace."

"Are you finished mocking me, dear?" asked Grandma Helen, her brow arched. "It was a harrowing experience, Christine, and one in which I have no intention of repeating, so if you don't mind, I'd like to just focus on my lunch."

"You know, I was actually surprised to have found a few cute things in there," I said. "I have some money saved up from babysitting, so I may actually go back up there and buy some of them."

"Oh, and where is that, dear," asked Grandma Helen.

"Uh, Walmart," I said, a little unsurely.

"No, darling, absolutely not," she shook her head vehemently. "I'll not have my only granddaughter dress in Walmart clothes."

"You know, mom, there's nothing wrong with buying clothes from discount stores," said Aunt Christine. "Ollie and I have found some great deals at Costco; In fact, their workout clothes, leggings, and yoga pants are well made and can rival some of the more expensive brands, so why not save the money?"

"Costco?" she shrieked. "Oh darling, you two really have sunk low into the depths." She lifted her hand to beckon Justin back over to the table, "It would appear I was mistaken, darling, I will be needing another one of these after all."

CHAPTER SIXTEEN

It was Friday night, and the impending family Christmas tree trimming party was finally upon us. Grandpa Anthony had spent the entire afternoon making homemade pizzas, and the smell of his hard work was currently wafting throughout the house. Dusty and I had opted to sit in the living room along with Ezra and Sabrina, while Aunt Christine, Brian, and the rest of the family were sitting around the kitchen table discussing salient topics, such as the proper use of ranch dressing. In the entire time that Ezra and Sabrina had been dating, he hadn't once brought her home to meet my parents, and in all honestly, I completely understood where he was coming from. Truth be told, I wasn't quite sure I wanted to involve Dusty in the lunacy of our family either, but I figured it would be in my best interest to at least introduce him to the circus, giving him a chance to flee, in case things were to ever evolve between us.

"You know, I really think I'm just going to stop putting ranch dressing on my pizza," said Beau, dunking a sizeable slice into the creamy dressing. "It tastes too much like a salad."

My mother, utterly perplexed by the statement, stared back at him in confusion, and was just about to say something when dad quickly interjected, "Don't," he said, shaking his head slowly. "Don't even try to make sense of it. You'll only drive yourself crazy; just get off the train now."

"It truly is an abomination, dear, it always has been," said Grandma Helen. "I'm honestly quite surprised your mother even allowed it to go on for as long as she did."

"And what would you have had me do, mother, starve him?" asked mom.

"Not starve him, dear, just maybe not enable him to make such poor food choices in the future," she answered dubiously.

"I'm not an enabler, mother," said mom, rolling her eyes. "And since when is putting ranch on pizza considered to be self-destructive behavior, anyway? The word 'enabling' is primarily used for things more sinister in nature, like alcoholism and drug addiction, so I would hardly categorize ranch on pizza as being anywhere in the realm of those two things."

"You say tomato, I say tomato," she shrugged.

Not quite reading the conversation of the room, Brian happily chimed in with, "You know, I've recently found that I actually like putting ranch on my-"

"No, Brian," whispered Aunt Christine, effectively cutting him off with an imperceptible shake of her head. "Don't say what you're going to say."

"On your what, dear?" asked Grandma Helen.

"Uh, cucumbers," he said, somewhat unsurely. "I like it on my cucumbers...and with...uh, carrots."

"Well, I suppose there's no accounting for taste, but at least that makes some semblance of sense." She dabbed at the corners of her mouth with her napkin, "I just don't understand the appeal of putting that insipid condiment on everything; it just seems so uncouth and uncivilized."

"Gee, grandma, don't feel like you have to hold back on our account, tell us how you really feel," said Beau.

Grandma Helen has always had a deep-seated hatred for ranch dressing, and none of us seem to know why. Not only does she despise it, but she also considers it to be a personal affront to all things Italian. So, by gently redirecting Brian from openly admitting to everyone that he loves dousing his mozzarella sticks in the aforementioned condiment, Aunt Christine saved us all from having to endure a lengthy diatribe on salad dressing etiquette, and more importantly, enabled him to retain his high Grandma Helen rating of approval.

Now, many of you may think that I'm over exaggerating, but I want you to understand that this is the same woman that used to taunt my friends whenever they came into the restaurant for not eating their entire meal. My poor friend Tara still has flashbacks of her interrogation tactics for not having finished her birthday tiramisu four years ago. You see, Tara was not a fan of anything coffee-flavored, so when Grandma Helen surprised her with a big slice of tiramisu, she politely took one bite and then hid the rest of it in her napkin, making it look as though she had finished it. Unfortunately, Tara wasn't very adept at hiding things well, so once her deception was uncovered, all hell seemed to break loose, and the interrogation began. To this day, she refuses to come over to my house for fear of dredging up old memories and/or running into my lunatic of a grandmother.

"Hey, when are we going to get this shindig started?" asked Ezra, bringing his empty plate into the kitchen. "Bree and I are hoping to make a late-night movie."

I quickly followed suit and was stacking our plates in the sink when mom said, "Well, why don't all of you start unpacking the decorations while Christine and I clean up." She stood from the table and began collecting plates. "Your father was kind enough to help me put the lights on earlier today, so at least you won't have to worry with that."

"Not by choice, mind you," he muttered under his breath.

Upon noticing mom's death stare, he quickly amended his statement by saying, "I mean, happy to help, dear!" He then took his leave from the table and headed into the living room to turn on some Christmas music and to light a fire in the fireplace.

As the four of us headed back into the living room, mom gently pulled Ezra over to the side, "Ezra, honey, you really need to shave."

"No, I don't want to," he answered plainly.

"Well, don't you think your girlfriend would appreciate you being clean shaven and hygienically presentable?" she asked.

"Nah, I think she's good with the way things are," he smirked.

"Yeah, well, you look like the human adaptation of Shaggy," she snarked.

"Ruh-Roh," he said, jokingly raising his brows.

"That's Scooby, smart ass," she said.

"Forgive me, dear mother, what I believe I meant to say was, Zoinks!" he said, letting his voice go up a few octaves.

"Are you finished mocking me?" she asked.

He walked over and lovingly put his arm around her, "Sorry, mom, it's hard to keep up with all your childhood cartoons that aired over half a century ago."

She jabbed him playfully in the ribs, "It's a good thing I love you, you know that?"

"Yeah, well, I'm very lovable," he grinned.

"Hey, we could really use your height in there," smiled Sabrina warmly, as she strolled up next to Ezra. "None of us can get anywhere close to the top without a ladder, and then it dawned on me that there was a 6'8" human ladder standing here in the kitchen, so I decided to come and get you."

Ezra bowed his head gallantly, "As you wish."

Completely taken aback with the ease in which he happily acquiesced, mom said, "So, what are the chances of me getting that kind of response when I ask you to do things?"

"Slim to none, my lady" he said over his shoulder.

"Well, at least I know I can count on you," she retorted sarcastically.

"You know, he only does that because he knows my favorite movie is "*The Princess Bride*," giggled Sabrina dismissively. She glanced over at the mess in the kitchen, "Is there anything I can help you with, Mrs. Jenkins?" She gestured over to the pizzas sitting on the counter, "I'd be happy to put the leftovers away in Tupperware, if you'd like."

"No honey, we've got this," said mom. "You go on and help the others with the tree… and please, call me Olivia."

"Yes ma'am," she said. "Oh, and by the way, I just wanted to let you and Mr. Jenkins know how grateful I am to have been included in your family festivities tonight. The food was beyond amazing and your home is absolutely beautiful."

"Thank you, honey, I appreciate you saying that," smiled mom warmly. "And always know that you're welcome here anytime."

Aunt Christine sidled up to mom and leaned in, "Oh, that girl is smooth," she whispered. She then raised an inquisitive brow, "Tell me, have we made a new friend?"

"She's a sweet girl, Christine," said mom, walking back into the kitchen. "I'm really hoping she'll be a good influence on Ezra; he hasn't always had the best luck when it's come to the opposite sex." She watched as Sabrina carefully unwrapped an ornament, "I'm really hoping this one is different."

"Yes, well, let's not forget that good influence over there also gave your son a bright red hickey a few months ago, as well as a few other things you probably haven't been made aware of," she smiled smugly.

"I'm well aware of that, Christine, thank you," she muttered. "I really don't need you pointing it all out to me every five minutes."

"Well, just know that I'm here if you need me," she smirked.

***

"Jingle bell, jingle bell, jingle bell rock
Jingle bells swing and jingle bells ring"

Grandma Helen was in an incredibly festive mood, dancing and singing merrily around the living room, while jubilantly sipping her third mug of dad's famous Peppermint Schnapps hot chocolate. The rest of us, however, were doing our best not to throttle her every time she corrected us on ornament placement and tree trimming etiquette.

"Snowin' and blowin' up bushels of fun
Now the jingle hop has begun"

Stepping up behind me, she said, "Oh, Addie, darling, that ornament doesn't go there, maybe put it down more toward the bottom."

"Dancin' and prancin' in Jingle Bell Square
In the frosty air"

She then gleefully danced over to my left, "Oh, Dusty, let's not put that one on the tree, dear, it's rather dull and doesn't really match with the others."

"What a bright time, it's the right time
To rock the night away
Jingle bell time is a swell time
To go glidin' in a one-horse sleigh"

She was shimmying merrily across the living room when a flat plastic ornament Sabrina was holding caught her eye, "Oh, no, dear, we don't use the ones that the children made in Sunday school." She took away Ezra's reindeer handprint and replaced it with a Christopher Radko handcrafted toy soldier, "Here, this one's much more elegant, not to mention more pleasant to look at." She watched closely as Sabrina carefully placed the ornament up on the tree, and then joyfully resumed her singing.

> *"Giddy-up jingle horse, pick up your feet*
> *Jingle around the clock*
> *Mix and a-mingle in the jinglin' feet*
> *That's the jingle bell*
> *That's the jingle bell*
> *That's the jingle bell rock"*

She was still dancing and singing merrily when she stopped abruptly, took a few steps back and said, "You know, the more I look at this tree, the more I think it isn't very straight."

"It's fine, mom," said Aunt Christine.

"No, I don't think it is, dear," she cocked her head slightly, "I think it's leaning a little too much to the right."

"Have some more Schnapps, Helen" said dad, patting her back, "I'm sure that'll help straighten it up."

"Ooh, yes, let's make me another one of those!" she exclaimed giddily. She looked over at Grandpa Anthony, who was contentedly scrolling through his phone, and lifted her mug exuberantly, "Honey, our marvelous son in-law is going to make me another one of these thingies, isn't that wonderful?"

"Yes, that's wonderful, dear," he grinned. "Just remember your ibuprofen and water before bedtime."

"Don't worry, darling, I'm not planning on getting inebriated," she waved him off.

"A little late for that," he muttered.

"What was that, dear?" she asked.

Grandpa Anthony's reply was immediately drowned out by squeals of delight as Grandma Helen watched Dusty unwrap her favorite ornament depicting Betty Boop popping out of a large colorful gift box. She leapt greedily at him, trying to take the decoration out of his hand, "Let me see! Let me see!"

"I'm sorry, did I do something wrong?" He nervously looked over at me, unsure of what was happening, "I didn't break it, did I?"

"No, honey, you're fine," said mom. "Just keep doing what you're doing." She looked over at Grandma Helen with a tight smile, "Mother, may I talk with you?"

"Later, dear, I'm about to put up my special ornament," she said.

"It's important," said mom, through gritted teeth.

"Ugh, fine," she sighed. She dangled the ornament from her finger, "Dusty, darling, would you please make sure to put Betty up in the top center portion of the tree, I want to make sure that everyone sees her at eye level."

"Uh, yes, ma'am," he smiled meekly. He hung the ornament and then looked quizzically over at me, "Please tell me I'm not supposed to know who Betty is."

Mom led Grandma Helen over to the other side of the room and spoke in a low voice, "Listen, I need you to take it down a notch," said mom. "You're acting like a crazed hyena."

"I most certainly am not," she said indignantly. "And I really don't appreciate your comparing me to such an ugly and rabid animal."

"Yes, you are, and for people that don't know you, it's quite unsettling," replied mom.

"You told me to be festive and agreeable, Olivia, and that's exactly what I'm doing," She started ticking off her fingers, "I haven't told Sabrina that the color peach looks terrible on her and that she seriously needs to rethink curtain bangs, I haven't mentioned Dusty's filthy blue jeans and severe need for a haircut, and I haven't even said one word about Brian's complete inability to hold a wine glass properly, so you see, I have been nothing but courteous and nonjudgmental, a feat, I'll have you know, that you know is quite difficult for me."

"You scared poor Dusty half to death, mother!" she hissed. "I mean, you practically mauled the kid for God's sake."

"Okay, yes, I may have been slightly eager to get my hands on that particular ornament, but it is my favorite, after all," she answered penitently. "And if it makes you feel better, I'll make sure to apologize to him later."

"You won't mean it," said mom.

"You're right dear, I won't," she winked.

She sauntered happily over to where dad had just set down refilled mugs of hot chocolate and picked one up, "Yay, more adult beverages!" She took a small sip and then asked, "Now, who wants to hear me sing *Santa Baby*?"

"How about *Grandma Got Run Over By a Reindeer*?" asked Beau.

"*Free Bird!*" yelled out Ezra holding his hand in the standard rock'n'roll salute.

"So tell me, is your family always like this?" asked Dusty.

"Unfortunately, yes," I sighed.

"That's awesome," he smiled.

Chapter Seventeen

The next morning, mom walked into the kitchen to find Ezra sitting quietly at the counter eating a bowl of cereal. He was scrolling through his phone and texting with someone, so he wasn't aware that she had walked up behind him.

"Good morning, honey," she yawned, kissing him on the back of his head, "Who are you chatting with so early in the morning?"

"Morning, mom," he said. "I was just texting with Bree about what we're going to do today."

"Oh, yeah, and what's that?" she asked.

"I think we're going to get some of our Christmas shopping done," he said, talking around a mouth full of cereal. "I was planning on heading downtown to pick up a few things from Retro Records, so we just thought we'd go ahead and grab some lunch, and maybe check out a few of the other shops while we're down there."

"What are you needing from the record shop?" she inquired.

"I ordered a few records for Beau that I know he's been wanting, and then…well, let's just say I'm planning on getting a little something special for grandma," he smirked.

"What in the world would grandma want from the record store?" asked mom.

"*The Carpenters Greatest Hits*," he deadpanned. "I know she's been dying to get her hands on a vinyl pressing."

"Are you out of your mind, she'll kill you!" she exclaimed.

"Relax mom, it's just a gag gift," he laughed. "I'm also planning on getting her a big box of those Belgian chocolates she loves so much, so I'm sure all will be forgiven."

"Well, just don't expect-" her words got stuck in her throat as she stepped into the kitchen and immediately caught sight of the mess surrounding her, "For the love of God, why?"

"Why what?" asked Ezra, not bothering to look up from his bowl.

"Why do you people insist on being such slobs?" She picked up an empty sleeve of Ritz crackers, holding it up for him to see, "And please explain to me why it is you people can't even be bothered to throw anything away."

"Hey, that's not mine," he said defensively.

"You know, every morning I come into this kitchen and spend at least 30 minutes cleaning up before I can even sit down and enjoy my morning cup of coffee," she said irritably, filling the coffee pot with water. "I honestly think it's time I just start charging everyone in this house a non-negotiable clean-up fee."

"Mother, surely you jest," he quipped.

She silently presented the entirety of the kitchen as if she were showing off the winnings of brand-new car, "Am I?"

"Well, it wasn't me!" he exclaimed.

She picked up the plastic microwave cover lid to show him the caked-on food inside, "Really?"

"Okay, that may have been me," he conceded.

He watched intently as she silently began to point out all of her other grievances; crumbs on the stove, a giant mustard stain on the counter, scattered food debris in the sink, dried up milk in the bottom of a glass, and a crushed sandwich bag box wedged inside a half-opened drawer.

"I'm sorry, I don't speak mime," he said casually, returning his attention back to his cereal bowl.

"Ezra, all of this may not be your doing, but I do know for a fact that this milk encrusted glass, here, is yours," she said, lifting the glass from the sink.

"Oh yeah, and how do you even know it's mine?" he scowled. "Last time I checked we had six people living here."

"Because this has been your calling card ever since you could drink milk out of a glass, son." she said. "Each one of you has a calling card that lets everyone know where you've been. Your brother's is leaving the toilet seat up, your sister's is leaving items of clothing all over the house, and yours, my darling boy, is dried up milk in the bottom of a glass."

He opened his mouth to object, but then thought better of it, "Yeah, well, at least I don't take the last of something and then leave the empty box sitting in the pantry."

"No, that would be your brother, and ever since I made him sit through a 30-minute seminar on the dos and don'ts of pantry etiquette, we haven't had that problem." She cleaned the crumbs off the counter and rinsed out the sink, "And if you don't want to have to sit through one, yourself, I would highly suggest you start doing what I'm asking you to do."

"I will have you know that I did empty the dishwasher the other day without even being asked," he retorted. "That was three minutes of my life that I'll never get back, thank you very much."

"You mean yesterday when it was just the cups being washed and nothing else?" she asked. "You poor thing, that must have been unbelievably daunting for you."

"Look, I just came down here for a bowl of cereal, I really don't want to get into an argument with you," he said.

"That's because you know you will lose," muttered mom.

As she waited for the coffee to brew, she pulled the creamer out of the refrigerator and changed the subject, "Hey, I'm curious, are you having any issues getting into Netflix from your TV?"

"No, why?" he asked.

"Well, the password doesn't seem to be working and I can't seem to figure out why," she said.

"Um, yeah, that's probably because I changed the password the other day when we were arguing; try Momsucks24/7," he said casually.

"Are you serious, right now?" she asked.

"With a capital 'M,'" he said with a self-deprecating smile.

"You are unbelievable, you know that?" She slowly poured cream into her mug, eyeing him as she did, "I can't believe I willingly shared my body with you for nine months."

"Hey, you and dad should have thought about that before deciding to throw caution to the wind like you did," he snickered.

"What are you talking about, you weren't unplanned," she said indignantly.

"I know, I'm just yanking your chain, mom," he winked. "What were you trying to watch anyway? I thought you were all about Johnny and Tara and the whole Grand Prix ice skating thing right now."

"I've been watching that, yes," she said. "But I've also been wanting to watch *A Castle For Christmas* with Brooke Shields," she clarified.

"Ew," he curled his lip. "Had I known that's what you were planning on watching I wouldn't have told you I changed the password." He got up, rinsed out his bowl, and made a grand gesture of placing it in the dishwasher, "Please take note, dear mother, that I am cleaning up after myself."

"Yes, darling, duly noted," she nodded. "And Ezra, change the password to something less obnoxious, please."

"As you wish," he bowed slightly, before bounding up the stairs.

Smiling to herself after hearing him utter the exact same words he had said to Bree last night, she poured herself some coffee and headed into the living room to light up the tree. She had just sat down on the couch and was serenely sipping her coffee when Aunt Christine shuffled drowsily into the kitchen.

"Good morning," said mom.

"Morning," she answered.

She poured herself some coffee and then came into the living room, plopping down unceremoniously on the couch next to mom, "Tell me, do you think the people working at Pinterest ever laugh at all of the crazy things people pin?"

"I can't say I've ever really given it much thought, why?" asked mom.

"I don't know, I was just scrolling through some of my pins and wondered if they thought I was slightly deranged, that's all." She pulled up her Pinterest page and presented it to mom, "Corn dip, pumpkin fudge, shrimp alfredo, chocolate peanut butter brownies, five cheese Italian pasta, and a size 2 pencil skirt I can't even fit my left thigh into; all of which were pinned, mind you, after stuffing my face with pizza."

"It's the holidays, I think we all tend to get a little over exuberant with our Pinterest pins," laughed mom. "And if that's the only toxic trait you have going for you, I think you're going to be just fine."

"Actually, I'd have to say my toxic trait is having a personality that alternates between 'I need to save money' and 'you only live once' and never quite knowing which one is going to show up on any given day," said Aunt Christine bluntly.

"Well, at least your able to admit and accept that about yourself," said mom. "That's certainly admirable."

"And what would you say your toxic trait is?" asked Aunt Christine.

Mom pondered the question a few moments before answering, "I really don't think I have any."

"Ha, yes you do!" answered dad, joining them in the living room. "You're toxic trait is not letting anyone else clean because you don't consider it clean unless you clean it, and then getting mad when no one offers to clean because of it." He kissed her on the head, "Oh, and also coming in behind us to clean what we've already cleaned up because it's not been cleaned to your specifications."

"Don't you have somewhere you need to be?" asked mom irritably.

"No, just here with my lovely wife, correcting her whenever she makes untrue statements about herself," smiled dad.

While mom and dad were bantering back and forth, I stormed downstairs in a fit of rage holding a handwritten note that had been taped on top of the upstairs toilet.

"He did it again, mom," I said. "He clogged up the toilet and this time he left a note." I handed it to her, "Please, for the love of all that is Holy, do something about your son."

Mom looked down at the note and then began to laugh, "Please don't use me!" it said, "I'm feeling a little under the weather :(."

"Mom, it's not funny!" I said. "He does this all the time."

Aunt Christine looked over mom's shoulder and read the note, "Okay, that's actually pretty funny."

"You'll only encourage him if he finds out you laughed at this, Aunt Christine," I said bitterly.

"Honey, I understand your frustration," she soothed, "but he's only making light of the situation, that's all."

"That's easy for you to say, you don't have to share a bathroom with him," I fumed.

Mom handed the note to dad, "Here, you may want to go find out what's happening with the toilet."

He snickered after reading it, "Well, at least the kid knows how to handle things with a little panache." He looked back over at mom, "I suppose I'll go figure out what's going on."

"I see you still have the atomic bomb sitting atop your head, Addie," snarked Beau as he waltzed carelessly behind me. "Why do you wear all of your hair on top of your head like that, anyway?"

"Shut up, Beau!" I said.

It's a simple question, there's no need to get your panties in a twist," he smirked.

"Beau would you mind telling us what exactly happened upstairs?" asked mom.

"I don't know what happened, the toilet just keeps getting clogged," he shrugged innocently.

"Well, son, your timing couldn't be more perfect" said dad clapping a hand on his shoulder. "Now you can go and get the plunger from the garage and meet me upstairs so we can figure it out together."

"What? Why?" he gasped.

Dad silently handed over his note, "I believe you know why."

"Ew, but the toilet is so gross, dad!" he shuddered. "I don't want to have to touch that thing; I could contract a virus that could kill me in two days or I could wind up suffering from some sort of man-eating bacteria."

"Son, just because you're capable of imagining stupid doesn't mean you have to bring it to fruition," said dad, beckoning for him to follow. "Come on, it'll be good for you to learn something new."

"But I'm on Christmas break!" he bellowed, following obediently after him. "My brain is already swimming in an endless sea of boring information, I don't need to add to it!"

"Yes, well, we all have things we don't want to do, dear," said Grandma Helen, taking a seat across from mom and Aunt Christine.

She clasped her hands primly on her lap and then cleared her throat, "Listen, darling, I think I've decided that I'm going to be needing a few dozen of those potato chip thingies you like to make. You're still planning on making those today, yes?"

"Potato chip cookies?" clarified mom. "Yes, I am, but I don't think I have enough ingredients to make any extra batches."

"Well then, we'll just have to make a quick little jaunt over to the grocery store, now won't we?" she chirped happily.

"Mom, I really don't want to have to add any extra work for myself today, so if you're wanting some, you're just going to have to help me," said mom.

"Yes, I figured you'd say something like that," she sneered.

"Why exactly do you need them, anyway?" I asked.

"Well, little miss Jingle Bells has decided to ask everyone to bring a special homemade treat for all the kids attending the event next week, and since I'm technically helping to plan this whole thing, she's now expecting me to help with all of the refreshments too."

"Who, Joan?" asked Aunt Christine.

"Yes," she snarled. "You know, I really need to remember to never do anything like this again, it's just too...cumbersome."

"You mean effectuating a charitable act and participating in something bigger than yourself?" asked mom sarcastically. "No, of course not."

"You wouldn't understand, Olivia," she said. "Everyone is constantly wanting something from me and none of them will leave me alone until they get it. It's exhausting, incommodious, and incredibly time consuming." She heaved a heavy sigh, "I think I just need a leaf blower, but for people."

"That's one I haven't heard before," snickered Aunt Christine.

"Alright, listen," said mom, "if you're willing to help make all of these extra cookies, I'm willing to go with you to the store to get what we need." She went into the kitchen and rinsed out her cup, "Just give me a few minutes to get dressed."

"Oh, that's wonderful, darling," she clapped excitedly. "You know, you may want to think about putting some make-up on too, you never know who you might run into."

"No, mother," said mom. "I have too much to do and not enough time to do it in, so you're just going to have to slum it today."

"Well, I suppose I'll just have to wear my oversized black sunglasses to avoid any embarrassment, dear," retorted Grandma Helen acerbically.

CHAPTER EIGHTEEN

"That is the last time I ever let you drive my car, mother!" fumed mom, setting the groceries down on the counter. "I cannot believe you left my car running with the keys in the ignition the entire time we were in the store; I just thank God we live in a low crime neighborhood."

"Yes, well, had you not been yelling at me about hitting pedestrians, none of that would have even happened," replied Grandma Helen. "The man was jaywalking, Olivia, he was practically asking for it."

"Do you ever listen to the words that come out of your mouth?" asked mom. "You could have killed a man today, mother!"

"Oh, I didn't even come close to hitting him, darling, you're overexaggerating like you always do," she waved away the concern. "And the whole key in the ignition issue was simply because you stormed out of the car before I even had a chance to turn it off and I was racing to catch up with you." She pulled out her phone to check her messages, "And yes, I may have been a little distracted and forgot to take the key with me, but nothing bad happened, so you see, it's all fine and well."

Mom stared dumbfoundedly at her, "No, mom, it's not fine, that's the whole point."

"It certainly sounds like you two had fun at the grocery store," said Aunt Christine walking into the kitchen.

Mom pulled out a large pineapple from the bag and placed it on the counter, "And don't even get me started on what you did with the pineapple, mother," she glared at Grandma Helen.

"Oh, it was all in good fun, Olivia," she snickered. "You're always so uptight, you really need to think about loosening up a bit."

"What's the deal with the pineapple?" I asked.

"Would you like to tell her, mother, or should I?" asked mom.

"I'm happy to leave that to you, darling," she smiled.

"Yes, well, apparently, a pineapple strategically placed in the left-hand corner of your shopping cart at the Publix up the street, means that you're...let's see how should I word this...oh yes, promiscuous, indiscriminate, and completely open to being solicited." She continued to unpack the groceries, "So, imagine my surprise at being lewdly propositioned by a man I have never met before while your grandmother slinks away behind the banana display to laugh at my complete and utter discomfort and embarrassment."

"Ew, gross," said Aunt Christine. "How did that even happen in the first place?"

"Well, while my back was turned, little miss mayhem and madness over here decided to wreak a little havoc, and unbeknownst to me, drop a three-pound pineapple into the front of my cart." She stopped unpacking groceries and glowered over at Grandma Helen, "I still can't believe you did that to me, mother; you are truly mentally depraved."

"You know, it could have been a lot worse, dear," she said, grabbing a bottle of water from the refrigerator.

"And what, pray tell, could be worse than being propositioned for sex in my local supermarket?" asked mom.

"Well, I could have done what Sheila did to her daughter, Misty, and flipped up your mailbox flag on a Saturday night," answered Grandma Helen.

"And what exactly does that do?" asked mom.

"Let's just say that Misty and her husband had a few unplanned visitors who were specifically looking for a swinging good time," she smirked.

"Um, what are you even talking about, grandma?" I asked.

"Orgies, dear," she said nonchalantly. "You wouldn't believe how many people around here participate in such debauchery."

"How is it you even know about these things?" asked Aunt Christine.

"Roberta tells me," she shrugged innocently. "You wouldn't believe some of the perverse and twisted things that poor woman has had the misfortune of witnessing while patrolling the neighborhood."

Roberta Howard, self-professed neighborhood know-it-all and all-around meddlesome busybody is the leader and sole member of our nonexistent neighborhood watch, a responsibility she took on shortly after her husband, Frank died. A widower for over ten years, she spends her days and nights sitting by her front window documenting the comings and goings of everyone in the neighborhood and has even gone so far as to conduct a few stakeouts from time-to-time in her 1991 Buick LeSabre. You see, Roberta has a slightly over-the-top obsession with police procedural television, so in order to manifest her lifelong fantasy of being in law enforcement, she now spends much of her time canvassing our neighborhood in search of anything that one might view as vulgar, unlawful, or scandalous.

"Mrs. Howard is 80 years old and stirs up trouble like a muckraker, you really can't believe everything she says," said mom.

"Oh, really?" she raised a brow. "How do you think I found out about Christine's little indiscretion earlier this year?" She took a sip of water, "Imagine my surprise at receiving an early morning phone call alerting me about my eldest daughter's single lady strut up the driveway." She looked over at Aunt Christine, "That was a fun little chat."

"Ugh, Mrs. Howard," she growled angrily.

"And that little pineapple in the shopping cart trick certainly seemed to work, so I'd say she probably knows more than you think she does," smirked Grandma Helen.

You know what, I'd really rather not talk about Mrs. Howard anymore," said mom. "Let's just get started with the baking, shall we?"

"Yes, let's do that, dear," said Grandma Helen amiably as she pulled down two wine glasses.

"Are you really planning on drinking wine while we do this?" asked mom.

Grandma Helen laughed heartily as she reached for the bottle of merlot sitting on the counter, "I don't know about you, darling, but I have absolutely no intention of doing this sober." She poured two rather large glasses of wine and handed one over to mom, "You know how much I despise baking."

Aunt Christine heaved a heavy sigh and stood to leave, "Well, as much as I would love to stick around and watch this week's episode of Blundered & Blitzed, I told Brian I'd meet him for lunch over at The Mill." She grabbed her keys off the counter and waggled her finger at them, "And you two, need to not to kill each other today, okay?"

She then sidled up next to me as I was placing cooling racks on the table, "Hey, do you think you're going to be able to handle Lucy and Ethel over there by yourself?"

"They'll be fine," I laughed. "Go enjoy your lunch with Brian; if they get too out of hand, I'll just hide the wine."

I watched as Aunt Christine walked out the door and then headed back into the kitchen, "Hey mom, just let me know what you need me to do. I have a few hours to help, but then Dusty's going to be coming by, if that's alright."

"Sweet, little Dusty," mused Grandma Helen. "He truly was a lovely boy, dear; quite charming and polite. I just wish we could do something about his name."

"Stop, mother," warned mom.

"I said he was a lovely boy, Olivia, I just don't care for the child's name, that's all." She sipped her wine and then sweetly tucked a strand of hair behind my left ear, "I don't know, darling, I just don't see you with a Dusty, I see you with more of a Sebastian or a Declan; you know, someone with a more regal sounding name."

"I like Dusty's name, grandma, it fits him perfectly," I said irritably.

"Well, that's unfortunate," she muttered into her wine glass.

"Okay, so here's the recipe," said mom, handing a notecard over to Grandma Helen. "It's a relatively simple one to follow, with very few steps, so you shouldn't have too much difficulty with it." She then looked apologetically over at me, "Addie, honey, would you mind putting on some Christmas music?"

"Nothing too somber, dear," called out Grandma Helen. "I'm drinking and need something peppy while I spend the day toiling in the kitchen with your mother."

"Yes, ma'am," I said.

"Toiling? That's a bit overly dramatic, don't you think?" asked mom. "Last time I checked, you were planning on helping me make Christmas cookies, not digging ditches in a prison chain gang."

"Well, I may as well be, dear, you know how much I hate working in the kitchen." She poured herself another glass of wine and sighed deeply, "So tell me, what exactly are you needing me to do?"

Mom pulled the standing mixer out from under the cabinet and plugged it in, "Do you think you can handle measuring out the potato chips?"

"Why don't you measure out the potato chips and I'll play with this thingy?" asked Grandma Helen as she randomly and giddily pressed buttons.

"Because you don't know what you're doing," said mom, slapping away her hands.

"Party pooper," she pouted petulantly.

Mom placed four sticks of softened butter into the mixer, "Addie, honey, would you mind getting the powdered sugar set up so we can sprinkle the cookies once they're on the cooling racks?" She reached into a drawer, pulled out a gallon sized Ziplock bag, and handed it to Grandma Helen, "It's going to work better if you put the chips in here. I think the recipe calls for two cups, but you may want to double check that before you measure."

Mom was slowly adding flour to the butter mixture when Grandma Helen dutifully held out her Ziplock bag full of chips, "Here you are, darling."

"The recipe calls for crushed potato chips, mom," she said. "Would you mind going back and doing that?"

"Well, won't the mixer do that for me, dear?" she asked.

"It's honestly better if they're crushed, they'll mix in easier and you'll be able to put in more." Mom opened a drawer and pulled out rolling pin, "Here, you can use this to crush them into smaller pieces."

"Or I can simply do this," she said brightly, as she dumped the entire contents of the bag into the mixing bowl. "Now, where's my wine?"

***

Three hours later and we were still working in the kitchen when Beau came downstairs for a snack.

"Hey mom, did you see the toilet sitting outside?" he asked. "Dad's fixing the leak upstairs, so he decided to set it upside down in the yard. Mrs. Simmons is having an absolute hissy fit! Although, honestly, I must say I think it adds a little something extra to our outdoor Christmas decor." He grabbed a granola bar from the pantry, "I was telling dad that

123

we should seriously consider buying an extra toilet so that we can decorate it in lights, and then have Santa sit on it while he reads the paper. Wouldn't that be funny?"

"I highly doubt the rest of the neighborhood would appreciate that, Beau," said mom. "Not everyone has your aberrant sense of humor."

"I think the world would be a better place if everyone did," he quipped. "Wait, what does aberrant mean?"

"Something that is different from the norm or atypical." She kissed the top of his head, "And yes, I agree with you, the world would most definitely be a better place." She handed him a plate filled with cookies, "Here, have one, I know you're working hard up there with your dad."

"Thanks, mom," he smiled.

"So, exactly how many more batches of these whatchamacallits do we actually have to make?" slurred Grandma Helen slightly as she carelessly slapped spoonfuls of dough onto a cookie sheet.

Mom surveyed the filled cookie tins stacked across the counter and on the table, "I think one more batch after this should be enough."

"Ugh, just because you like people enough to go through all of this tedium, doesn't mean I do," she snarled. "Why don't we just buy a few dozen cookies from the bakery, darling, and just be done with it?"

"Because it's Christmas, mother," said mom. "A time when we deliberately go out of our way to deceive others into thinking we're more festive and jovial than we actually are."

"Uh, mom," interrupted Beau, spitting out his cookie, "I hate to tell you this, but these things taste really nasty."

Chapter Nineteen

Mom immediately grabbed a cookie from the plate she had just offered to Beau and took a bite, "Oh my god, these are awful." She then handed the cookie over to Grandma Helen, "Here, taste this."

"I'm not about to bite into that," she curled her lip. "Why is it that people always insist on making other people taste things that they know are going to taste bad. I mean, why would anyone knowingly and willingly succumb themselves to sampling something that they know is going to be unpalatable? It makes absolutely no sense to me."

"Mother, what exactly did you do?" asked mom.

"Why in the world would you be blaming me, darling?" she sounded bewildered.

"Oh, gee, I don't know, maybe because you are, after all…you," she answered.

"You know, I really don't appreciate being held accountable when there are three of us working in this kitchen today," she huffed irritably.

"I'm holding you accountable because you're the one that insisted on taking over the dough so that you could, and I quote, 'play with the mixer and pretend that you were a contestant on *The Great British Baking Show*.'"

"Well, I must say, it is a wonderful show, dear, and one I think you might find very informative," she said matter-of-factly.

Mom crossed her arms and spoke quietly, "Please tell me you're not watching Acorn TV again."

At the beginning of last year, Grandma Helen purchased a monthly subscription for Acorn TV, a streaming service that offers access to television shows from Britain, Ireland, Australia, and beyond. She would spend every night glued to the TV watching anything and everything made available to her. This is also where she learned to hone her flawless British accent, by the way; a talent she loves to flaunt whenever she and Grandpa Anthony visit King George Tavern, a local English pub and eatery that many true British transplants tend to spend a good bit of time in. This obsession with British television eventually transferred over into everyday life when she became fixated on the show, *The Madame Blanc Mysteries*. The story follows an antique dealer that moves to the south of France after finding out that her late husband squandered all of their money in secret, but the thing that affected Grandma Helen the most, was not the plot of the show, but rather the way the main character would always refer to someone as "love." Knowing her penchant for latching on to all things absurd, it's really no surprise that the woman spent the entire second half of 2022 calling everyone she came in contact with, "love." It drove my mother absolutely crazy, so the disquieted statement about watching Acorn TV was not at all unwarranted.

"No, love, I'm not," answered Grandma Helen in a British accent.

Just then a slew of colorful obscenities emanated from the upstairs bathroom where dad was working.

"Welp, duty calls, I suppose," shrugged Beau nonchalantly.

"Son, where are you? I need your help!" yelled dad.

"I'm coming, dad!"

"Hey, bring me a few cookies, would you?" he shouted from the top of the stairs.

"I honestly don't think you want me doing that!" he answered.

"What, why not? Tell your mother that we are not giving all of those cookies away; I want some too!"

"I think someone needs to be careful about what he's wishing for," sang out Beau as he climbed the stairs.

"Where are the cookies?" asked dad, meeting him halfway.

"Trust me dad, I just saved you from something extremely unpleasant, so please feel free to go ahead and up my Christmas endowment this year because I definitely deserve it."

As soon as dad and Beau were back upstairs, mom returned her attention to Grandma Helen, "Did you even read the recipe while you were mixing the dough?"

"Kind of," she said.

"What exactly is that supposed to mean?" asked mom.

"Well, I had a bit of an unfortunate incident while you and Addie were upstairs helping Greg," she said.

"What kind of unfortunate incident?" reiterated mom.

"I spilled my wine, dear," she said.

"Okay, well, you obviously cleaned everything up, so, what's the problem?"

"On the recipe card," she murmured.

"I'm sorry, could you say that a little bit louder please?" asked mom.

I spilled my wine on the recipe card," she sighed.

"And you didn't think to tell me this until now?" shrieked mom. "That was two hours and God knows how many batches ago!"

"Well, I'm the one who's wine spilled, darling!" exclaimed Grandma Helen indignantly. She picked up the bottle of red wine sitting on the counter, "Now I'm left having to drink this cheap Two Buck Chuck swill from Trader Joes that you and your sister have become so accustomed to."

"Oh, my God!" said mom as she began pacing the floor. "I have absolutely no idea which tins have the tainted cookies, and other than sampling each one, there is no way to find out." She looked over at Grandma Helen, "Do you have any idea how much time, ingredients, and money we wasted because you wouldn't tell me the truth?"

"Well, when you put it that way, darling, you make it sound much worse than it actually is," she scoffed. "Let's try thinking positively, shall we?"

"Think positively? Mom, I have absolutely no idea which cookies are good and which are bad, and even if we sampled one from every container, that still won't guarantee that there aren't defective ones mixed in." She put her hands on her hips and looked around at the stacks of brightly colored tins, "We're just going to have to throw them all away, I guess."

"You know, dear, we can always have the bakery downtown make some for you," offered Grandma Helen. "I'm sure Mimi would be more than happy to dumb down her cookies and make some less than stellar one's for you to claim as your own."

"Oh, and how exactly would you like me to pay for all of that, mother, shells and beads?" asked mom.

"Oh, now don't start throwing all that anthropological stuff in my face, darling, you know how it bores me." she bristled. "Good God, I still remember having to listen to your stories of the Yum Yum people and how they bartered with their tribal neighbors for food and supplies."

"That's the Yanomami people of South America, mother, and none of that even matters right now, so let's just focus on the issue at hand, okay?" said mom.

"Actually, mom, I think I can sort everything out," I said excitedly.

I walked over to the stack of tins sitting on the counter, "I remember filling all of these up first and then moving them over here to clear room on the table for the empty ones. I did all of that while you were showing grandma how to work the mixer, so I'm pretty sure that the cookies grandma made are the ones sitting on the table right now and the good cookies are the ones sitting up here on the counter."

"Oh, Addie, I love you so much!" said mom, letting out a grateful breath. She quickly came over and hugged me, "You have no idea how happy I am that you were here to help with all of this, sweetheart, thank you."

"What a wonderful Christmas miracle, darling," said Grandma Helen jovially.

Mom opened one of the tins and sampled a cookie, "Yes, these taste so much better, thank you Lord!"

"Hey, mom, I think Dusty's going to be here soon, do you mind if I go upstairs and get ready?" I asked. "I had planned on helping you and grandma clean everything, but he's about to be here."

"Baby girl, you go and do whatever you need to do," smiled mom. "You helped me in more ways than you will ever know, and for that, I owe you." She reached for her wine glass in celebration, "Go have fun with Dusty, just be home by 10:30."

"Thanks, mom," I said. "I love you both."

"Love you, darling!" called out Grandma Helen. She then walked over to the kitchen counter and visibly took in the sea of cookie tins laid out before her, "So, which ones are mine?"

"Oh, no, you're not going to get off that easy," said mom. These are all mine; I don't know what you're going to do."

"Well, that's certainly no way to spread holiday cheer, dear," she scowled.

"Need I remind you that we're in this predicament because of you?" asked mom. "You're the one that messed everything up in the first place."

"Well, you let me do it!" she exclaimed.

"Yes, mother, and against my better judgement, I might add," she said.

"Well, what am I supposed to do now?" she lamented. "I told Joan I was going to bring a big batch of our family's famous potato chip cookies to the Christmas celebration on Tuesday; I can't not show up with them, I've been telling everyone how delectable they are."

"Technically, they're not our family recipe, mother, you know this." She raised her brow, "You've got to stop telling lies."

"It's not a lie, dear, it's semantics," said Grandma Helen. "Greg is married to you, which makes him my son in-law, which means that we are family, and since family shares everything, the famous potato chip cookie recipe is now forthrightly mine."

"You know, in your dementedly warped and twisted mind I can actually see how that might make sense to you," snarked mom.

"Say what you want about me, Olivia, but I could really use your help with this, please," she said somberly.

Mom took one look at the sadness in Grandma Helen's eyes and immediately regretted what she had said. "Okay, fine. I'll help you make one more batch."

"Oh, wonderful, darling," she said brightly. "I'll pour the wine!

***

"What in the world happened to you?" asked dad. "You look like you've been run over by a Mack truck." He took a seat at the end of the couch and gently pulled mom's legs into his lap, "Is it your mother?"

"When is it not my mother?" asked mom.

"Do you want to talk about it?"

"Not really," she sighed.

"Okay," he smiled.

"Well, it's not entirely my mother," she grumbled. "It's really more about my consumption of way too much cookie dough, cookies, and sugar today that my body is now screaming, 'My God, woman, try eating a salad to redeem yourself.' But rather than listen to it, I've chosen to

129

allow my son to eat fruit out of a can while I lay here and contemplate making it a 'fend for yourself' night so that I can stuff myself with Publix buffalo chicken dip and drink beer. I think I've hit a new low."

"Well, if it makes you feel any better, I think we're supposed to have a white Christmas," said dad.

"Are we really?" she perked up. "That'll be nice. Maybe it will snow so much that my mother won't be able to get out of her house."

"We're in Georgia, honey, I don't think we're going to get the same amount of snowfall that they do in New Hampshire," he laughed.

"Hey, thanks for fixing the toilet upstairs," said mom. "I know that's not something you really wanted to do on your day off."

"Well, Beau was actually a big help, so it made things a lot easier." He snuggled in close, "Listen, why don't you go grab yourself a beer and that buffalo chicken dip you were talking about, and I'll order a pizza and rub your feet tonight."

She pulled him in close and sultrily said, "You, my good sir, have just earned yourself some major bedroom points tonight."

From the other side of the Christmas tree, gagging sounds erupted from Beau as he said, "Ugh, somebody stop this planet, I want to get off."

CHAPTER TWENTY

"Why do I have to take Churchill for a walk in the freezing cold while you get to stay in a nice warm house?" asked Beau, as he zipped up his winter coat.

"Because you are the child, and I am the parent," said mom. "And I've recently come to the realization that my sole purpose for living is to make your life miserable, so there's that too."

"Ugh, I can't believe this!" he bellowed. "I'm like a bondservant."

"Beau, let me ask you something," she said. "Who is it that helps you with school every day? Who buys your video games? Who takes you to basketball practice? Who feeds you?" She crossed her arms in front of her chest and raised her brow, "Better yet, who sat here patiently this morning listening to you drone on and on about how crawfish make the perfect meal because they consist of both a little bit of meat and a little bit of drink?"

He stared vacantly at her for a few seconds and then deadpanned, "I have absolutely no idea."

"Listen, do me this favor and I will make you a grilled peanut butter and jelly sandwich while you're gone, okay?" she appeased.

"I see we've taken to bribery now, but my stomach is betraying me, so I guess I'll have to agree to the terms and conditions of the contract being offered." He grabbed the leash off the counter, "Come on, Churchill, let's make this quick."

Just as Beau was heading out the back door, Grandma Helen sidestepped inside, careful to avoid being marked upon by Churchill's slobber. Although he is not the most affectionate dog, he certainly seems to like Grandma Helen, and despite her many attempts to avoid him, he always seems to seek her out above anyone else. You see, Churchill is a smart dog, and knowing his personality as we do, we honestly think he gravitates to her simply because he knows that she doesn't like him. As a result, she is often the one he chooses to direct the majority of his attention and unwanted advances to. Regardless of why he does what he does, it drives Grandma Helen absolutely crazy, and that, I think, is pretty much the point, at least as far as Churchill's concerned.

"Hello dear," she said, taking a seat at the kitchen counter. "Would you mind pouring me a cup of coffee with my special creamer?"

"You mean Baileys?" asked dad, coming in from the laundry room.

"Ooh, now there's an idea," she cooed. "Yes, that would be divine, darling, thank you." She looked adoringly over at him, "Oh, Gregory, whatever would we do without you?"

"The list is long, Helen," he winked.

He walked over to mom and held out a large clump of lint, "One of your children is not cleaning out the lint tray before starting the dryer, any idea which one?"

"I have my suspicions," said mom, "but I'll see what I can find out." She poured coffee into a mug and then added a splash of Baileys, "Here you go, mom."

"A little chintzy on the Baileys, dear, don't you think?" criticized Grandma Helen as she peered into her cup.

"A little early to get sloshed, mother, don't you think?" countered mom.

"Touché, my darling," she smiled.

Grandma Helen watched as mom pulled out the peanut butter and jelly to make Beau's sandwich, "So, Olivia, did you get my message about your father playing Santa Claus for the Angel tree celebration?"

"Yeah, I did, but I thought he and his friends were visiting the children's hospital that afternoon," she said. "Do you really think he's going to have time to make it back up here after being down in Atlanta all day?"

"Oh, he'll probably be cutting it close, dear, yes, but he said that he shouldn't have any problem making it here in time." Grandma Helen sighed contentedly, "I tell you, that man is an absolute Godsend; I really don't deserve him."

"And you're only now coming to this realization?" murmured mom, under her breath.

"Anyway," continued Grandma Helen brightly, "Now that your father has graciously stepped up to play the role of Santa, I no longer need to rely on Myron to do it, thank God."

"Myron, the one that flirts with you all the time?" asked mom.

"Who's Myron?" I asked coming into the kitchen. "That's not a name I've heard you mention before, grandma."

"That's because I try not to, dear," she said. "Olivia's right, though, he is a bit sweet on me, but that's not why I didn't want him to do it."

"What's wrong with Myron?" asked dad.

"Well, Myron tends to love his Christmas cordials a little too much, dear, if you know what I mean." She took a sip of coffee, "At last year's Christmas party, he got rather inebriated and ended up completely stripping down backstage before running the entire length of the theater yelling out, "naked run.""

"Oh, dear God," said mom, squeezing the bridge of her nose.

"Well, the first few laps were actually rather funny, but then it got old, and we just ended up going back to our conversations; it really wasn't all that exciting," she shrugged.

"So, he was completely naked?" I asked.

"Well, not completely, dear, no, he was still wearing his little elf hat with the jingle bells, although that eventually came off too as he tried seeing if a certain part of his anatomy would work as a hat rack. Either way, his shenanigans really didn't seem to bother anyone, but I just don't want to have to take that chance with all the news cameras around, you know?"

"So no one even cared that he was streaking?" asked dad surprised.

"We're theater people, darling, we're nothing if not eccentric," she answered flippantly. "Besides it takes a lot more than an old shriveled up—"

"Okay, well, I need to head over to Home Depot for a few things," interrupted dad.

As dad was kissing mom goodbye, Beau walked in from outside, "Okay, listen, if Mrs. Bartlett says anything about Churchill's indiscretions with her poodle, I want you to know that I really did try to intervene." He took the leash off and walked into the kitchen, "And I'm just going to go ahead and state for the record that Churchill can do a lot better than Lulu, that dog is just not attractive."

"Well, she certainly makes a better alternative than that hideous pillow lying on his bed," said Grandma Helen, rolling her eyes.

"Oh, he's simply upgrading, that's all," said mom. She handed Beau a plate, "Here's your sandwich, honey."

"Thanks, mom" he smiled.

Dad buttoned up his coat and grabbed his keys "Hey, bud, I have to head over to Home Depot; you want to come with me?"

"Yeah, I do!" He grabbed a paper towel and wrapped it around his sandwich, "Bye mom, bye grandma!" He started toward the door and stopped short, giving me a sidelong glance, "Goodbye sibling."

"Ugh, can't we just please sell him, already, mom?" I growled.

"He'd only be returned to us, honey, so it really doesn't even make sense to try," she sighed. Would you like me to make you a grilled peanut butter and jelly sandwich?"

"No, I'm good, thanks," I said.

"Why didn't you ask me if I wanted one, dear?" pouted Grandma Helen.

"I did once, and you likened it to peasant food, so I figured you wouldn't want to offend your opulent palate with such unpleasantness," answered mom matter-of-factly.

"Oh, yes, that's right, I did," she mused. "Yeah, no, I don't want any."

"Okay, bye, mom, I love you," said Ezra, bounding down the stairs and into the kitchen.

"Where are you off to?" asked mom.

"I have to go help Mark with his truck, but I should be home in time for dinner." He pulled on his coat, "What are we having anyway?"

"Salmon, rice pilaf, and broccoli," she answered. "And remember, Nana and Pops are coming over tonight too."

"Okay, well, I'll try not to be late, but if I am, would you mind saving some salmon for me?" he asked.

"Please stop pronouncing the "L" in salmon," she sneered.

"What, that's how I say it," he snickered.

"No, you don't, you've been taught better than that, Ezra" she combated.

"I think what your mother means to say, dear, is that you sound like a complete and utter moron, and that it drives her insane," offered Grandma Helen. "Isn't that right, darling?"

"Moron, cretin, idiot, any one of those will work," she grumbled.

"I know, that's why I do it," he winked.

"Oh, hey, before you go," said mom walking around the kitchen counter, "I need to know which one of you is putting your clothes in the dryer without cleaning out the lint tray. Your father amassed a rather large quantity of lint while putting the towels in the dryer for me this morning and he was not happy about it."

"I always clean the lint tray, mom, you know this," I said. "Ever since you told me how dangerous it is, I always make sure to empty it."

"Well, don't look at me," said Ezra indignantly. "I barely wash my clothes as it is."

"Look, I really don't care who it is, I just want it to stop," said mom. "When not cleaned out properly, a full lint tray can start a fire, so either text yourself a reminder, place a note on the dryer, or phone a friend and have them remind you, I don't care, just start cleaning out the lint tray."

"But all three of those things would require forethought, mother, and that's really never been my strong suit, you know this about me," deadpanned Ezra.

"How do you know it isn't Beau," I asked.

"Because Home Economics doesn't start until next semester for your brother, and more importantly, I'm not financially ready to risk the well-being of my washer and dryer quite yet." She walked back into the kitchen, "And, just like your grandmother, he's not to be trusted with large appliances."

"It was the one time, Olivia," said Grandma Helen irritably. "How was I supposed to know that dish soap and dishwashing detergent are two separate things?"

"Oh, I don't know, maybe because I spent ten minutes explaining the differences to you?" asked mom.

"Yes, well, I lost interest after a few seconds and immediately began drowning you out with a mental rendition of ABBA's *Dancing Queen*," she smirked. "I tend to do that whenever I'm bored."

"Okay, well, I really have to go," said Ezra.

"Just please try to be home by 6:30, okay?" asked mom.

"I'll do my best," he smiled, kissing her cheek. "Bye grandma, Bye Addie."

"Goodbye, darling," waved Grandma Helen, before finishing the last of her coffee.

She returned her attention over to mom, "So, tell me, exactly when are you expecting your father and me to show up for this thing you're forcing us to come to tonight?"

"You mean the gift exchange with George and Carol?" clarified mom.

"Yes, that thing," she curled her lip. "I don't understand why can't we just wait until Christmas Eve like we always do?"

"Because it's supposed to snow that night, mom, and they don't want to have to risk driving in dangerous conditions."

"Well, you do have three children that can be expelled from their rooms, darling," she smartly pointed out. "Just ask them to spend the night here."

"We did offer for them to stay here, but they both said that they would prefer being at home if the weather gets too bad," said mom. "You know how dangerous winter storms in North Georgia can be."

"A valid point, I suppose," she shrugged. "Just please tell me she's not planning on giving us all paintings for Christmas; I don't think I can easily get away with hiding another one of those things."

"It's what she does, grandma, it comes from her heart," I smiled.

"Yes, well, why can't her heart at least point her in the direction of an Elizabeth Arden gift certificate? A facial, I can use, but another one of those wildflower paintings is both immoderate and overly excessive, if you ask me."

"So, what did you end up getting Nana for Christmas, then?" I asked.

"A season pass to the theater," said mom, rolling her eyes. "Because that's not at all immoderate and overly excessive, now is it, mother?"

"Of course, it's not, dear," she grinned.

CHAPTER TWENTY-ONE

"George and I just want to take a moment and thank y'all for taking the time to celebrate our family Christmas early," drawled Nana, her small frame eclipsed by the towering fireplace standing behind her. "I know this wasn't what y'all had planned for tonight but we're just so thankful to each and every one of you for taking time out of your busy schedules to attend this little impromptu get together."

"Why is everyone else's Christmas present in an envelope while mine is in a giant rectangular box?" whispered Grandma Helen as she leaned in close to mom. The two of them were sitting next to each other on the sofa listening to Nana as she addressed the room. "I just know it's another one of those damn farm paintings," she spat. "Ugh, the cross I bear for this woman."

"Shh, mother, stop, please," said mom.

"The minute George and I learned that there would be a winter storm heading our way on Christmas Eve, we knew that we were going to have to make a quick change of plans," continued Nana.

"I don't want another painting, Olivia!" she hissed.

"You're acting like a child, stop," muttered mom.

"We just love y'all so much and wanted to make sure that we still had the opportunity to celebrate Christmas with you, even if it meant having to do it a little bit earlier than originally planned," smiled Nana.

"I'm pretty sure everyone else is getting a gift certificate except for me," sneered Grandma Helen.

"Must you do this right now?" asked mom irritably.

"And it was also important to us to be able to give you your presents beforehand, just in case we weren't able to see you on Christmas morning," smiled Nana.

"You know what a gift card says, Olivia? It says, 'Here, you do it, because I don't want to.' It's the epitome of lazy," she scowled. She looked despondently down at the large festively wrapped box in front of her, "Quite honestly, though, I'd gladly welcome a Dairy Queen gift card right about now if it meant not having to accept another one of those god-awful wildflower paintings; I hate farm décor, you know this."

"I swear, mother, if you don't stop this nonsense, I'm seriously going to come unglued," warned mom.

"Okay, well, I'm just babbling now, so I'll just go ahead and stop talking so y'all can open your gifts," said Nana. "Merry Christmas, everyone!"

"Merry Christmas, y'all!" exclaimed Pops, taking a seat next to her.

While everyone was excitedly tearing into their envelopes, Grandma Helen continued to sulk in her seat, dispassionately taking in the enthusiasm and exuberance of everyone around her.

"Open your gift, mother," said mom, through gritted teeth.

"Just give me a minute, will you darling, I'm mentally preparing myself for all the lies I'm going to have to tell," she snapped.

"A $200 Visa gift card, thanks Nana, thanks Pops!" exclaimed Beau, running over to give them each a hug. "Now I can buy that new game controller I've been wanting and some of the DLC's I need."

Aunt Christine held up a small brown gift card, "Oh, my goodness, thank you. Brian and I absolutely love The Cheesecake Factory." She smiled warmly over at the two of them, "Thank you so much for thinking of us."

"Happy to do it, darlin," winked Nana.

"Oh, wow," exclaimed dad. "A Smoking Pipes gift certificate, thank you so much!"

"We want you to use that to buy the pipe you've been wanting for so long," said Pops. "It won't cover the entire cost, but it should pay for most of it."

"It's the perfect gift, thank you so much," said dad.

"See, I told you everyone is getting a gift card except for me," growled Grandma Helen.

Mom opened her own envelope and smiled widely at the $200 Amazon gift card laying inside, "Oh, wow, thank you both so much, this is so generous of you." She lifted it up for everyone to see, "I know exactly what I'm going to get with this."

"Well, Greg told us that you were wanting a bigger air fryer, and since I wasn't sure which one you wanted, I thought a gift card would make things a little bit easier," grinned Nana.

"Oh, yes, this is perfect, thank you," smiled mom.

"I'd happily take an air fryer over what's sitting in this box," mumbled Grandma Helen irritably.

"You will accept whatever it is graciously, do you understand, mother?" said mom, lowering her voice. "And stop being rude, it's Christmas for Christ's sake."

Ezra and I opened our envelopes and immediately ran over to thank Nana and Pops for our Visa gift cards, while Grandpa Anthony beamed down excitedly at the Harley Davidson gift card he was holding in his hands. "This is fantastic, thank you!" he said. "They're actually a few accessories I've been thinking about getting, so this will definitely help me out with all that."

Once everyone had opened their gifts and the excitement had dissipated, Nana began picking up the discarded pieces of wrapping paper that was laying on the floor. She immediately noticed that Grandma Helen had not yet opened her gift, and quietly approached her, "Helen you still haven't opened your gift, is everything alright?"

Mom nudged Grandma Helen slightly, "Of course it is, she's just saving the best for last, right mom?"

"Uh, yes, dear, exactly," she said, lifting the large box onto her lap. "I think I just got lost in all the revelry and was so engrossed in everyone else opening their gifts, that I completely forgot about my own."

This, of course, was a bold-faced lie. Anyone who has ever met the woman knows that she has never, and will never, take interest in someone else's prosperity above her own. In fact, the whole "It is better to give than to receive" concept is completely lost on her, so to hear her say these words is very much akin to hearing someone say that the Titanic never sank, it's a complete and utter fabrication.

Grandma Helen reluctantly began unwrapping her gift with a look of apprehension painted plainly on her face. She slowly released the last piece of tape and then began painstakingly folding the paper into a small succinct square, a behavior completely out of character considering she usually rips wrapping paper to shreds before mutilating the package underneath. She then opened the cardboard box and carefully peeled back the layers of tissue paper before letting out a surprised gasp. Inside the box, she saw a beautifully painted framed Tuscan landscape staring back at her. The painting depicted a prodigiously large stone Tuscan villa flanked by a multitude of Large Italian Cypresses, and the sky, made up of resplendent gold and orange hues, complimented the verdant green leaves found in the rows of grapevines lying in the foreground. It was truly a beautifully painted picture, and the fact that Grandma Helen knew immediately that it would fit perfectly in her Italian themed home, was a true testament to Nana making the right choice in not presenting her with a gift card.

"Carol, I don't know what to say," said Grandma Helen, obviously taken aback. "This is absolutely stunning; I can't believe you painted this."

"Oh, I'm so glad you like it," she beamed. "You know, I was actually painting the ones that you—" she stopped midsentence, as if realizing she wasn't supposed to say what she was about to say, "Uh, I mean, I was painting one of these for another friend of mine, and just thought you might like to have one too."

Grandma Helen looked oddly uncomfortable for a moment, but then quickly regained her composure, "It's gorgeous, Carol, I absolutely adore it!"

"Carol, you really outdid yourself with this one," said mom, staring longingly at the painting. "The colors are so rich and vibrant; it makes me feel like I'm actually there." She took a deep breath and smiled, "Oh, what I wouldn't give to be able to see the rolling hills of Tuscany someday."

"Yes, well, that probably won't be happening anytime soon, dear," snickered Grandma Helen. "But, if it's any conciliation, we can always drink like we're in Italy!" She clapped her hands excitedly, "Let's go get the wine!"

"Hey mom, are we still going to do family game night?" asked Beau. "You said we might be able to play a few rounds of Headbands if it wasn't too late, and since it's only 8:00, I figure we can still get in a quick game or two."

"Is that the silly little game you like to play with on your phone, dear?" asked Grandma Helen.

"Yeah," he smiled. "You really liked it, remember?"

"Tolerated is more like it, darling," she quipped.

"As long as everyone's up for playing a round, we can certainly do that," said mom. "Let me just open a few bottles of wine and we'll see about getting started, okay?"

"Okay," smiled Beau. He looked over at Nana and Pops, "You are going to love this game, Pops, it's so much fun!"

"Oh, it sounds like a great time, darlin," said Nana sweetly. "Why don't you come show Pops and me how to play?"

Mom, Aunt Christine, and Grandma Helen walked into the kitchen and were lining up wine glasses when mom's shoulders sagged and she groaned irritably, "Ugh, please God, not right now."

"What's wrong, dear?" Grandma Helen looked over at mom, "Oh, darling, you're glistening, and not in a good way."

"Here, use this," said Aunt Christine, pulling a hair tie out of her pocket, "I always make sure to have one on me just in case I need it."

"Thank you," said mom gratefully. "I just get so hot and miserable every time this happens." She tied her hair back at the nape of her neck and reached for the wine opener, "Menopause sucks."

"Darling, you really may want to rethink the way you're tying your hair with that thing," said Grandma Helen. "It's entirely too low."

"I just need it off my neck so that I can cool down faster," said mom.

"I understand that, dear, but why don't you tie it up higher, maybe give it a little more volume," she clarified. "Low ponytails are simply not attractive."

"I'm not trying to win any beauty contests, mother, I just need to cool down." She picked up an envelope that was sitting on the counter and began fanning herself with it.

"Not looking like that, you certainly won't," muttered Grandma Helen.

"She's fine, mom," said Aunt Christine. "No one here cares about how she wears her hair, except for you."

"Well, she looks like one of our nation's founding forefathers," sneered Grandma Helen. "Very reminiscent of Alexander Hamilton, if you want to know the truth."

"I don't, mother," replied mom. "But thanks for the compliment."

"I was simply trying to help, dear, there's no need to get snippy," she bristled.

"If you really want to help, you can bring those wine glasses over here," said mom.

"Yes, dear," she sighed. She walked over to the glasses sitting on the counter, "Christine, darling, are you planning on participating this evening?"

"Uh, yeah, I think so, why?" answered Aunt Christine.

"Well, then, you may want to seriously consider serving white wine rather than red," said Grandma Helen, opening the refrigerator. She pulled out two bottles of chardonnay and set them in front of mom, "You know your sister's propensity to get out of hand when it comes to competition, dear. If she starts baby-fish-mouthing tonight, your living room floor is going to be in for a world of hurt."

To say that Aunt Christine gets a little bit out of hand during family game night is an absolute understatement, and her inherent ability to turn something fun and enjoyable into a violent scene from *Mortal Kombat* is truly a sight to behold. You see, whenever Aunt Christine engages in any form of match-type competition, she becomes overly crazed and starts yelling out her answers at decibel levels that really have no place in family game play. Mom says that she's been like this ever since childhood, and that it wasn't until the movie, *When Harry Met Sally* came out in the late eighties, that Grandma Helen was even able to coin the verb, "baby-fish-mouthing." I've honestly never seen the movie, but from what I understand, there is a scene where a group of friends are playing Pictionary, and while Sally (Meg Ryan's character) is drawing what looks to be a baby talking, Jess (Harry's best friend) calls out all sorts of crazy and unintelligible utterances, with baby fish mouth being one of them. Realizing there would never be any intelligible way to describe her daughter's outlandish game time behavior, Grandma Helen immediately chose to adopt and appropriate the fatuous phrase, thus making the term "baby-fish-mouth" a regularly used household expression.

"White wine it is," said mom, reaching for a bottle.

After the wine had been served and everyone was finally settled in to play the game, Beau handed his phone over to Grandma Helen.

"Okay grandma, you're up first," he said.

"Yes, darling." She held the phone up to her forehead and a picture of a nurse in blue scrubs came onto the screen, "Am I an animal?" she asked.

"No," answered everyone.

"Am I something that can be used outside of the home?"

"Yes," they nodded.

"Am I something that helps people?"

"Yes, definitely," they said.

"Oh, I know, I'm the perfect shade of lipstick!" she yelled out enthusiastically.

Chapter Twenty-Two

"What do you mean she has a bigger story to cover?" shrieked Grandma Helen. "She promised that she would be here, Tobias!"

"Simone had every intention of coming up here, Helen, but a major story just broke and she needs to cover it," he said calmly. He walked over to the large evergreen standing in the corner and straightened a few ornaments hanging from the front branches, "She said that she was incredibly sorry, but that this new story was really important and needed to take precedence over everything else."

"Well, then, can't someone else come here and do it?" She followed closely behind, careful not to step on the heels of his shoes, "Certainly there are other reporters willing to cover this story; I mean, it's Christmas for God's sake!"

"Simone was only doing this as a favor to me, darling," he said. "It was never even on the stations radar, so I completely understand her desire to focus on something bigger."

"Well, it's on my radar!" she exclaimed. "Do you have any idea of what I had to go through to even make this night possible?"

"Don't you mean all the things that Joan had to go through?" He turned and watched as Joan happily hung decorations across the stage, "You know, she's taken it upon herself to be here every day wrapping gifts for all of those kids. She's gone above and beyond and we really need to be respectful of that."

"Yes, well, let's remember that I'm the one that had to go to Walmart to buy all those gifts!" She lowered her voice, "Those children wouldn't even have anything to open if it hadn't been for me and my rebarbative day trip into the seventh circle of hell." She curled her lip and shuddered, "I'm still trying to shake off the trauma from that afternoon."

"Yes, well, I'm fairly certain that the four martinis you consumed at the Bistro immediately following your hellacious experience helped you to do that," he smirked.

"Tobias, you and I both know that there isn't enough alcohol in the world to expunge the vulgarity of that place," she combated.

"Look, Helen, there really isn't much we can do about it right now anyway, so I suggest we just continue along as if nothing has changed," he said. "Everything is going to work out just fine, darling, you'll see."

"But everything has changed!" she insisted. "That's the whole point."

"I'm sorry, darling, but you're just going to have to make peace with the fact that there will be little to no press coverage here tonight," he voiced quietly.

Grandma Helen immediately took leave from him and walked over to where mom and I were standing, "Well, I guess we're just going to have to kiss that televised opportunity goodbye." She picked up a Christmas stocking and began stuffing it with candy, "Now we're going to have to rely on word of mouth, and Lord knows that won't get us very far."

"I'm sorry, grandma, I know you were really looking forward to being interviewed." I said, kneeling down to grab a box of candy canes. "And who knows, maybe that reporter will come and do a different feature story next year that will bring even more attention to your theater group."

"It's not just that, darling," she sighed. "I was just really hoping that we would be able to shed a little light on the fact that even in a small-town such as our own, the effects of poverty and impoverishment are very common and prevalent issues."

"Wow, where's all this coming from?" asked mom.

"I know you think me heartless, dear, but I have been known to think about the well-being of others from time-to-time," she smiled. "You know, we had 25 children to shop for the other day, and from what I understand, that wasn't even a quarter of the families that reached out for help. If our small community has that many people in need, I can only imagine what's happening in the larger cities and towns." She set down the now filled stocking and picked up another one, "I was just hoping to be able to spread a little awareness and get more people involved, that's all."

"And that's honestly the whole reason you're upset?" probed mom. "There's nothing else driving this disappointment?"

"Well, that's about 30 % of it, dear, yes," she nodded.

"And the other 70%?" asked mom, her brow raised.

"Darling, have you seen how good I look today?" She turned around slowly, flaunting her new Chanel teal-colored pantsuit, "This color not only comes across great on camera, but really showcases the green in my eyes, and now thanks to Simone and her disruptive breaking story, hundreds of thousands of viewers across the state of Georgia will no longer be able to see me looking this fabulous, so yes, I am upset, and rightly so."

"Ah, there's the little disingenuous narcissist we all know and love," said mom.

"You know, Helen, I couldn't help but overhear your conversation just now," interjected Sally Henderson, the theater's communications liaison, "but I wanted to let you know, if it makes you feel any better, my nephew, Michael is planning on attending the festivities and will be writing up a story to share with his readers. I have no doubt that it will help bring in a little more awareness for what we're doing here."

"Oh, that's wonderful, dear," said Grandma Helen. "Tell me, is he with *The Atlanta Journal Constitution*?"

"Uh, no, nothing that big," smiled Sally.

"*Creative Loafing*? *The Marietta Daily Journal*?" she continued.

"Oh, heavens no, nothing like that," she giggled. "He writes for *The Hickory Briar Post*, a small paper up in Jasper."

"Jasper?" repeated Grandma Helen derisively. "You mean that godawful backwater town situated just north of us? Are they even big enough to warrant having a newspaper?"

"That's enough, mother," muttered mom quietly.

Before Sally even had a chance to respond, Joan walked deliberately down the aisle toward front of the stage, vocalizing the plan for the rest of the day.

"Okay, everyone, we really need to start getting this place looking like Santa's village," said Joan, clapping her hands for attention. "We only have until 5:00, so let's go ahead and breakup into teams so that we can narrow our focus a bit. Let's see, Sally, Lexi, and Arlene, you go and get the stage ready. Walter, you and Harold can get the tables prepped and ready for the refreshments, and Helen, you, Olivia, and Addie can decorate the Santa's workshop picture booth that's been set-up in the foyer. Tobias and I will be coming around to help wherever needed, so please don't hesitate to let us know if you require our assistance."

"You know, I can understand having a schedule in place and a plan laid out, but someone really needs to explain to that woman that there is a fine line between organization and fascism," hissed Grandma Helen.

"Joan is not a fascist," said mom. "She's a lovely woman that stepped up to the plate when no one else was willing to, so for her to take charge is not only fair, but completely expected."

"Fine, take her side, darling," shrugged Grandma Helen. "I'm sure Michael from the *Pickle Brine News* will do a lovely write-up showcasing all of her wonderful organizational skills."

"It's the *Hickory Briar Post*, mother," corrected mom.

"Hickory Briar, Pickle Brine, what difference does it make?" she quipped. "I'm sure that his millions of subscribers will thoroughly enjoy his enthralling story about Joan and all of her charitable deeds."

"That's not what any of this is about, and you know it," said mom. "And stop being hyperbolic, it's unnecessary and in poor taste."

As the three of us began to decorate the photo booth, Beau and Nana walked through the door deep in conversation about his ostensible claim that chocolate is just as healthy as any other vegetable simply because it is derived from a plant.

"You know, Nana, chocolate actually comes from the cocoa tree, which is a small evergreen tree native to South America but can also be found in parts of Africa and Asia," he said, helping Nana carry in a large platter of treats. "That means that it technically falls under the category of a plant, so essentially, one could argue that chocolate belongs in the same category as vegetables when referencing the food pyramid, and as such, should actually be considered healthy and good for you."

He set down the platter on a chair and immediately walked over to us, "Hey mom!"

"Hi, honey," she waved. "Hi Carol, how are you doing?"

"Hey, darlin, I'm just fine," she drawled. "We're just here to drop off these plates of chess squares and brownies, where would you like us to leave them?"

Mom pointed to the other side of the room where Walter and Harold were setting up banquet tables, "Uh, I think refreshments are being set up over there, so you should be able to leave them on one of those tables."

"Oh, hey mom," said Beau, "Ezra wanted me to tell you that he's been trying to get a hold of you, and that he wants you to give him a call as soon as you can."

"Oh, okay." She looked over at me, "Addie, honey, I left my phone in my purse and it's up on the stage, would you mind grabbing it for me, please?"

"Yeah, of course," I said.

Mom was in the process of laying out multiple wooden dowels decorated with paper Santa hats, beards, and reindeer antlers when I returned with her phone.

"Thanks, baby," she smiled. She quickly opened the phone and immediately dialed Ezra's number, "Hi, honey," she said.

"Wow, in the time that it took you to call me back, I could have been either kidnapped or killed, I hope you know that," he snarked.

"Sorry, I left my phone in my purse, is everything okay?" she asked.

"Oh, you mean you actually care about me now?" his voice went up an octave.

"Ezra, you're 6'8," no one in their right mind is going to risk getting caught abducting a man of your size, it just wouldn't be prudent," she said.

"Yeah, well, that's what chloroform is for, mother," he retorted sourly.

"Which means that the perpetrator would have to be able to reach your nose and mouth in order to even make that work, so I'm pretty sure you're safe," she rebutted.

"Not if I was sitting down and completely unaware that someone intended me harm," he countered. "I can't believe my own mother doesn't care about the well-being of her firstborn son, it makes me feel so used and unloved."

"Are you finished?" she asked.

"Oh, relax, mom, I'm just messing with you," he laughed. "Anyway, I'm calling because something's come up."

"Okay, what's going on?" she asked.

"Grandpa's been trying to reach both you and Grandma, and since he couldn't get a hold of either one of you, he called me." He paused momentarily, unease prevalent in his voice, "He said that his motorcycle is having issues and that he doesn't think he's going to be able to make it back up there in time to play Santa tonight."

"Please tell me this is another one of your jokes, Ezra," said mom without inflection.

"I'm sorry, mom, it's not," he said. "I'm actually driving into Atlanta right now to help him with all of this, and since dad's out of town and Aunt Christine is taking pictures for the Angel Tree celebration, he had no choice but to call me."

"Damnit," she muttered irritably. "Okay, well, just please promise me you'll be careful while you're down there and let me know what happens."

Mom ended the call and then sheepishly grinned over at Grandma Helen, "Addie, sweetheart, would you mind finishing up the photo booth while I discuss something privately with your grandmother?"

"Yeah, that's fine," I said. "We're almost done anyway."

"What seems to be the problem, darling?" asked Grandma Helen, allowing mom to pull her away from listening ears, "Please don't tell me your sister's done something foolish. Where is she, by the way? Did she remember to get the champagne for later tonight?"

"She'll be here soon, and yes, she remembered the champagne," said mom. "Listen, we have a slight problem, and I need you to stay calm. Do you think you can do that for me?"

"Well, that depends, how slight is this problem?" she asked.

Mom surveyed the area for prying eyes and ears and then quickly rattled off Ezra's message, the words tumbling out of her mouth so fast they hardly made any sense. Once she had finished, she immediately braced herself for the tsunami of emotion that was sure to erupt out of the small woman, but instead, she saw only confusion and perplexity staring back at her.

"Darling, please speak coherently, you're not a monkey," said Grandma Helen. "And try not to look so gauche while you say it."

Mom sighed heavily and pinched the bridge of her nose, "Okay, fine." She crossed her arms and pointedly looked down at her, "Apparently dad's motorcycle has broken down in downtown Atlanta and he doesn't think he'll be able to make it back up here in time for the party,"

"What?" she shrieked.

"Would you please lower your voice?" pleaded mom.

"I'm going to kill him, Olivia," she fumed. "How could he do this to me?"

"Mom, he didn't deliberately do this, you can't blame him for something he has no control over," said mom.

"I knew something like this would happen," she spat. "Will he at least be here in time to play Santa for my *Santa Baby* number?"

"I'm not entirely sure, Ezra's on his way to help him right now," answered mom.

"So now Ezra's going to miss my number too?" she cried out. "What am I supposed to do, Olivia? We have twenty-five families coming here in two hours to watch me perform. How exactly am I supposed to sing sultrily about desiring expensive presents to a vacant chair?"

"Okay, yes, I can see how that might concern you," appeased mom, "but I think the more pressing issue here is that we have no one to hand out presents to all those kids."

"What?" she asked in confusion.

"Those children are coming here and expecting to see Santa tonight, remember?" said mom. "That's the main attraction as far as they're concerned."

"Oh, yes, the children," she sighed irritably.

"Didn't you say there was someone else you had thought about asking to play Santa?" asked mom.

"Who, Myron?" asked Grandma Helen. "Ugh, please don't make me call him, dear."

"I don't think we have much of a choice in the matter, mom," she said. "He's the only other person we know with a Santa suit."

"Fine," she relented. "But beware, if he hasn't stayed out of the brandy today, we're all in for a world of hurt."

CHAPTER TWENTY-THREE

It was 5:30 and we were still waiting for Myron to make his grand appearance as Santa. The families had started to arrive, and the excitement emanating from the kids and their parents was a wonderful sight to behold. The photobooth that had been set up in the foyer was a big hit, and since Aunt Christine was gracious enough to volunteer her time and talent and offer free family photos to any and all who wanted them, the line for it was incredibly long. Brian, who was happily playing the role of assistant, wrote down names and email addresses and handed out props, while mom and I manned the refreshments, making sure greedy little hands did not abscond with all the various treats laid out on the table.

We had just shooed away two young boys when we saw Grandma Helen walking over to us, painstakingly doing her best to avoid the children running wildly around her. "You know, one would think that these children would have some sense of decorum and appropriacy, but no, they're acting like little barbarians running around causing chaos and mayhem everywhere they go; it's truly appalling behavior and their parents should be ashamed."

"They're children, mother," shrugged mom. "It's what they do."

"Yes, well, I can assure you that you and your sister would never have been allowed to act so egregiously." She slowly scanned the room, watching the children happily bounce up and down in the theater's seats, "Where are all of their parents, anyway; it's beginning to look like Armageddon in here, and last time I checked, I did not sign up to be a babysitter."

"Let them have their fun, mother," said mom. "I don't think these kids have the opportunity to participate in events like this very often."

As we stood watching the delirium unfold, a young girl with a chocolate-stained face walked up to Grandma Helen and gently tugged on her hand. Looking down, she immediately noticed that the child's hands and face were not only sticky, but covered in brownie crumbs, and hovering perilously close to her swanky new outfit.

"Ew, you're dirty, please don't touch me," implored Grandma Helen.

"Hi," said the little girl, completely unfazed.

"Hello," she answered stiffly.

"You're pretty," the girl smiled, stuffing the remainder of her brownie into her mouth. "I like your outfit."

"I'm sorry, what did you say, dear?" asked Grandma Helen. "I'm afraid I'm unable to understand you with that enormous piece of confection lodged in your mouth."

"She said she likes your outfit and that you're pretty, grandma," I said.

"Oh, well, um, thank you," she said awkwardly, taking a large step away from the child.

The young girl immediately followed suit, shortening the distance between them. She then reached out her brownie encrusted hand and tried to touch the pristine, teal-colored material of Grandma Helen's pantsuit.

"Oh, my god, what are you doing?" she asked in a panic, taking further steps away from the child. "Olivia, what is she doing? Why is she following me?"

"I want to touch it," said the young girl innocently.

"Have you completely lost your mind, this is Chanel," she shrieked. "Just go back to your mother, dear, I'm sure she's here somewhere."

"But it's so pretty," she persisted.

Grandma Helen, in an effort to evade the stained faced child, strode quickly over to the opposite side of the refreshment table, "It's also incredibly expensive and does not need your little chocolate handprints all over it!"

"Can I touch it if I wash my hands?" she asked, edging closer.

"Ho…Ho…Ho!" rang out a deep voice from the back of the stage, "Merry Christmas, everyone!"

"Santa!" the little girl's eyes lit up, as she abandoned Grandma Helen to join the group of boys and girls excitedly watching Santa descend the stairs on the side of the stage.

"Oh, thank God," sighed Grandma Helen gratefully, although I was unsure as to whether or not it was because Myron had finally shown up or because her suit was no longer in jeopardy of being blemished by tiny chocolate fingerprints.

"Myron, darling, meet me over by the tree!" she shouted over the hysteria erupting from the mini mosh pit gathering around him.

"You need to call him Santa, mother, not Myron," reminded mom.

"Oh, yes, I suppose that would be prudent, dear, wouldn't it," said Grandma Helen. She waved wildly in his direction, trying to get his attention, "Santa, darling" she trilled. "We really need you to go over to the tree and help us hand out presents!"

Myron continued to greet the children, completely oblivious to Grandma Helen and her request to hand out gifts.

"Santa, we need you over by the tree, dear!" she tried again.

Grandma, I don't think he can hear you," I said. "It may be better if you just let things settle down a bit before trying to hand out presents."

"Are you out of your mind, we have a schedule to keep," she hissed. "And I have absolutely no desire to be surrounded by these little monsters longer than I have to be." She turned abruptly, barreled her way through the ecstatic throng of children, and barked out, "Santa, tree, now!"

Of course, the moment she noticed all the parents shuffling into the theater, she quickly donned a spurious mask of enthusiasm and added sweetly, "These precious little children have been waiting anxiously and patiently for your arrival, so let's not make them wait any longer to see what you've brought for them." She clapped her hands excitedly and beckoned them all over to the corner of the room, where an enormously decorated Christmas tree stood, surrounded by dozens of festively wrapped boxes, "Come children, come and see what Santa's brought for you!"

"Um, what exactly is happening?" I asked.

"What do you mean?" asked mom.

"Why is grandma suddenly acting agreeable and child friendly?"

"Because there's an audience older than ten currently walking into the theater right now, and your grandmother is nothing if not mendacious, especially whenever she knows people are watching her closely," answered mom.

"Mendacious?" I furrowed my brow.

"It means untruthful, deceitful, and every inch the embodiment of your grandmother right now," said mom.

"Joan, darling, where are you?" called out Grandma Helen. "Has anyone seen Joan?"

"Here I am," said a voice from the far side of the room. She quickly made her way down the aisle and joined Grandma Helen in front of the tree, "Good evening, children," she smiled warmly. "We are all so excited to have you here to celebrate Christmas early with us, and I know that Santa is even more excited to be here to hand out each of your gifts personally, so without further ado, let's all give a warm southern welcome to our special guest of honor, Santa Claus!"

"Santa Claus! Santa Claus! Santa Claus!" chanted the children excitedly.

"Ho…Ho…Ho, merry Christmas, boys and girls!" he slurred slightly. He walked over to where Joan and Grandma Helen were standing, teetering a bit as he did, and draped his arms around them, "Well, I can see that Santa's two favorite helpers have been busy unloading his sleigh of goodies," he hiccupped. "I hope you remembered to lock it up; we don't want anyone taking it for a joyride, now do we?"

"Have you been drinking, Myron?" whispered Grandma Helen.

"Nope," he shook his head vehemently, and then held up a three-finger salute, "Scouts honor."

As Joan worked to settle the children down and patiently get them seated and organized, Grandma Helen irritably pulled the tipsy Santa out of earshot and laid into him, "If you screw this up, Myron, so help me God I'll—"

"Relax, Helen," he cooed, cutting her off with a wink, "Myron's the man with a plan, so no need to worry your pretty little head with any of this, it's all going to work out just fine, trust me." He bent down close to her and whispered, "You smell really good, by the way."

"Ugh, and you smell like a distillery, "she scrunched her nose in disgust. "Please, just tell me you're going to be able to handle this professionally, and that your clothes will remain buttoned, zipped, and snapped at all times this evening."

"Of course, I can," he slurred indignantly. He then smiled lasciviously and lowered his voice seductively, "And only if you want them to."

"Okay, Santa, I think we're ready for you," called out Joan sweetly. "I have your list right here, so let's go ahead and get started, shall we?"

"Listen to me," said Grandma Helen, quickly grabbing his arm. She pointed to the giant red chair surrounded by poinsettias and mini-Christmas trees sitting at the center of the stage, "While the two of us are up there, you will sit down, shut up, and smile. There will be no utterances, no ad-libbing, and no extemporization of any kind; do you understand me?"

"But I'm Santa Claus, he garbled incoherently. "I'm the main attraction."

"Not tonight, you're not," she snapped. "You will behave accordingly, and not embarrass this theater, have I made myself clear?"

"Ooh, I like a woman that takes charge," he grinned.

"Don't be repugnant, Myron, I'm happily married and not at all interested," she sneered.

She stalked back over to where mom and I were standing, "Addie, darling, would you mind grabbing your brother and helping to hand out gifts? I think Santa needs all the help he can get right about now."

"Sure, of course," I said.

"So, is it really that bad?" asked mom.

"Well, he seems to be functioning alright for now, but I really don't want to take any chances." She saw Brian standing in a doorway and waved him over, "Brian, darling, would you mind helping Olivia keep an eye on Myron? He's had one too many Christmas cordials today, if you know what I mean." She grabbed her garment bag, "Now, if you'll excuse me, I need to go and get ready for my performance."

"Who's Myron?" asked Brian.

"The inebriated, fat, jolly guy in the red suit over there trying to hand out presents," sighed mom.

"Hey, mom, is Santa drunk or is he just illiterate?" asked Beau sidling up next to her. "The guy can't read any of the names on the presents and he keeps toppling over into the tree every time he bends down, so I figure he's either drunk or stupid."

"Shh, keep your voice down," hissed mom. "Let's not announce it to the world, okay?"

"Oh my gosh, he is drunk, isn't he?" laughed Beau. "I'm telling you; grandma is going to freak when she finds out!" He walked away shaking his head in amusement, "And to think I didn't even want to come tonight."

***

An hour later, we found ourselves standing backstage watching Grandma Helen parade around channeling her best Eartha Kitt impersonation as she serenaded the crowd about being a good girl and wanting expensive gifts for Christmas. She was wearing a deep crimson, floor length gown with a slit up the side and a white feather boa draped around her neck. Myron, it would seem, had finally sobered up some, and even though he sat there motionless, he watched her intently, with a look that was both indescribable and somewhat disconcerting. I think he may have even been talking to her intermittently throughout the performance because she kept staring daggers at him whenever she turned to face him.

> "Santa Baby, just slip a Sable under the tree for me
> Been an awfully good girl…"

"Oh, yes, you have," purred Myron. "A very good girl, indeed."
She looked oddly at him, unsure of what he was saying, but then continued, taking her boa and wrapping it seductively around his neck.

> "Santa cutie, fill my stocking with the duplex and checks
> Sign your 'x' on the line
> Santa cutie, and hurry down the chimney tonight"

"You can slide down my chimney anytime," he murmured softly.
His sexual innuendo along with the salacious look in his eyes was enough to make Grandma Helen immediately back away from him, and rather than continue to serenade him as originally planned, she began strutting up and down the stage focusing her attention more on the audience, rather than him.

"What is she doing, that's not how I remember she and dad rehearsing it," said mom.

"I don't know, but something seems to be off," observed Aunt Christine.

"You know, it looks as if he might be talking to her while she's singing," said Brian. "And whatever it is that he's saying, I don't think she likes it."

"The man's wasted," shrugged Beau. "He's literally playing 'What's my name and losing,' so is it really all that surprising to you?"

Grandma Helen was finally nearing the end of her number, and while her intention was not to get too close to Myron, she became sidetracked with her boa and accidently stepped within arms-reach of him.

"Come and trim my Christmas tree
With some decorations bought at—"

Her words were immediately cut off as Myron greedily grabbed her and set her firmly on his lap, "I'll happily trim your tree," he slurred in her ear.

Rather than risk ruining the performance, Grandma Helen, being the consummate professional that she is, continued on as if nothing had happened. Once the final notes of the song had finished playing, she smiled radiantly at the crowd, waved to everyone, blew kisses, and then forcefully swung her fist down into Myron's crotch, rendering him both incapacitated and out of commission for the rest of the evening.

"Oh my gosh, did you see that?" yelled Beau, "I think grandma just slapped Santa's nuts!"

CHAPTER TWENTY-FOUR

A few days had passed since the memorable nut slapping event, and although Grandma Helen was completely over it, Grandpa Anthony was still harboring ill will toward Myron and his impudent behavior. It didn't matter that Myron had apologized profusely for his misconduct, nor did it matter that he was taking a self-imposed leave of absence from the theater to focus on his sobriety, his wife had been manhandled and disrespected, and he wanted revenge. Being the hot-tempered Italian he is, he came perilously close to castrating the poor fellow, and had it not been for Grandma Helen's composure and equanimity in the matter, he just may have. However, after much discussion and contemplation, she was able to help him see reason, explaining to him that Christmas was a time for forgiveness, and more importantly, that fine wine and good Italian food are not served in prison. Although, I personally think her vow to never step foot inside the disease infested conjugal accommo- dations provided by the state of Georgia is what really changed his mind. Regardless of the reason, the whole episode seemed to be behind them, and they were happily back to normal.

Tonight was Christmas Eve, and with all of us settled in for the night, mom offered to open a bottle of wine for everyone. We had just returned from the church's candlelight service, and dinner at our favorite downtown restaurant, Prime, when mom stepped into the kitchen to retrieve everything.

"Wasn't that a lovely Christmas Eve service?" asked mom. "Of course, I'd really appreciate it, Beau, if next time you refrain from using your Bible as a machine gun." She uncorked the bottle of merlot sitting on the counter, "I don't think Mrs. Kitterman really enjoyed you playing out your warlike fantasies during the choir's *Joy to the World* performance."

"I was actually channeling John Wick, but I can see how you might have gotten the two confused." He walked over to her as she was pulling down wine glasses, "So, mom, I was thinking about having mini corndogs for dinner tomorrow, unless you know, you're planning on cooking something and eating it is unavoidable."

Mom paused from pulling down the glasses and glared at him, "You can't possibly be serious right now."

"Oh, I didn't mean that in a bad way," he soothed. "I was just telling you my plans since you told me to let you know whenever I plan to eat something different than whatever it is you're making."

"Tomorrow is Christmas, Beau, and I'm sorry, but your aunt, sister, and I did not spend the entire day in the kitchen prepping for Christmas dinner for you to eat cheap processed meat covered in cornmeal batter." She set the last glass down on the counter, "We have traditions in this house, and one of those traditions is eating a labor intensive and operose Christmas dinner that is consumed in less than fifteen minutes, so no, you will most certainly not be eating corndogs for dinner tomorrow."

"Okay, fine, but I'll have you know that corndogs would be a perfectly acceptable Christmas meal in Cambodia," he countered.

"The Cambodian people don't even celebrate Christmas, dork," I denoted calmly.

"Exactly, thank you for proving my point," he smirked.

"You don't have a point, that's the whole point," I argued.

"I do too have a point, you're just too stupid to understand it," he spat.

"Okay, listen," interjected mom, "I need for the two of you to stop arguing and help me take these glasses into the living room. Grandma Helen and Grandpa Anthony want to give us all our gifts tonight, so let's not keep them waiting because the two of you can't get along."

"Um, will we still get to open one of our presents like we always do on Christmas Eve, or does opening their gift completely negate the one family tradition, besides sausage balls, that I actually enjoy?" asked Beau.

"Don't be greedy, Beau," she said. "I think you can wait until tomorrow morning to rake in all of your Christmas cache."

"Wait, I'm getting money too?" he asked excitedly.

"No, that's not the kind of cache I'm referring to," she shook her head. "You know what, never mind, let's just take all of this into the other room, and enjoy spending some time together as a family."

"Ugh, but I spend enough time with you people as it is," whined Beau.

"Look, this is important to your grandparents," said mom. "For whatever reason, they're wanting us all to open our gifts together, in a tranquil and peaceful environment, not during the Tasmanian Devil display you tend to demonstrate every Christmas morning."

"Hey, I take offense to that," he said indignantly. "I can't help that I get excited at the prospect of gaining new Xbox gaming arsenal; it's Christmas and I'm a kid, I'm supposed to act that way."

"Beau, darling, you're making it incredibly difficult for me to be the parent I've always imagined myself to be, right now, so please, in an effort for me to not kill you, do what it is I'm asking you to do," said mom.

"Yes ma'am," he yielded.

We followed mom into the living room, helping her hand out glasses of wine, and then sat down on the floor next to Churchill, who was snoring loudly, completely oblivious to everyone else in the room. I think he may have been exhausted from an earlier tryst with his pillow and was now sleeping off the peculiarly amorous encounter. Aunt Christine and Brian were snuggled up on the couch together, while Grandma Helen and Grandpa Anthony sat in two chairs across from them. Ezra and mom took up the other side of the couch, while dad sat comfortably in his chair, looking out the window at the large flakes of snow falling down on the ground.

"You know, I'm really glad we were able to make it home before the weather got too bad," he said. "If it keeps coming down like this, we should find ourselves waking up to a beautiful white Christmas in the morning."

"A white Christmas would be perfect," I smiled.

"Do you think we'll get enough snow to make a snowman?" asked Beau excitedly.

"Well, they're saying that we're supposed to get up to at least four inches tonight, so it's certainly a good possibility," said Brian. "I'm anxious to see how much we actually get, though."

"I'm just thankful we had the presence of mind to go to the store the other day and stock up on wine and champagne," said Grandma Helen. "I can't even begin to imagine being isolated for days on end unable to drown my crippling boredom in the glass of a good Bordeaux."

"Yes, well, with the amount of wine you purchased, mother, I highly doubt you'll ever have the chance to find out," snarked Aunt Christine.

"Well, as long as the snow doesn't tun to ice, we should be good in a day or two," said dad. "Snow tends to melt relatively quickly here in the south, so I doubt we'll be stranded for very long."

"I miss the snow we used to get back in Cleveland," mused Grandpa Anthony. He lovingly put his arm around Grandma Helen, "Back in those days, neither one of us had a desire to ever leave the house when it snowed because we were always finding interesting and fun ways to occupy the time, remember, honey?"

"That, I do, my darling," she patted his leg. "That, I most definitely do."

"Ew, I think I could have gone my whole life without ever having known that," said Ezra sarcastically, looking up from his phone.

"Look, I really don't care what happens, just as long as we don't lose power," said Beau nonchalantly. "I have a lot of video games to play over the next few days, so the weather really needs to cooperate." He pointed over to the tree where a wrapped box stood towering over the rest, "Plus, I'm banking on that big box in the corner over there being the new gaming chair I wanted, so, snow or no snow, as long as the power remains intact, I'm good with whatever happens." Realizing that everyone was still staring at him, he congenially added, "And, of course, spending Christmas with my family."

"Okay, well, enough of all of this bleak talk of snow," said Grandma Helen. "I think it's high time you all open your gifts. Ezra, darling, would you mind playing Santa and hand everyone their present?" She watched as he read the tags before diligently passing them out, "Now, it's extremely important that everyone open them at the same time, and once you do, I want you to turn them around so that everyone else can see what it is that you're holding."

"Well, this sounds interesting," said Aunt Christine.

"I have to admit, I'm anxious to see what's under the wrapping," said mom.

"Okay, now, before you all open your gifts," said Grandpa Anthony, "I want you to know that this is something your grandmother and I have had in the works for quite some time. We actually started discussing the idea a few years ago but didn't seriously begin planning anything until earlier this year."

"Now, Brian, darling, I hope you understand that this was all planned out before you and Christine started dating," said Grandma Helen. "We absolutely adore you, dear, but unfortunately, you're just a little too late to the party."

"I understand completely, Helen," he smiled. "There's no need to explain anything to me, I'm just happy to be able to share in the moment."

"That's a lovely sentiment, Brian," mocked Beau. "Can we please open our gifts now?"

"Yes, of course you can," laughed Grandpa Anthony.

We immediately began opening our gifts, some more delicately than others, I might add, and turned them around just as Grandma Helen had instructed us to do. Glancing around the room, I could see that each one of us had received the same small picture frame, but that is where the similarities ended, as each one was filled with a different painting portraying various locations found in and around Italy. For example, mom's painting depicted the rolling hills of Tuscany, while dad's showcased the towering Colosseum in Rome. Aunt Christine's painting consisted of the picturesque foothills of the Alps overlooking Lake Como, while Ezra's was a strikingly vibrant picture of Mt Vesuvius, and where Beau's frame revealed the quirky design of the Leaning Tower of Pisa, mine flaunted the colorful cliffside village of Positano.

"I don't understand," said mom, looking around the room at everyone's painting. "They're absolutely beautiful, but what exactly is the meaning behind them?"

Grandma Helen and Grandpa Anthony waited a few moments before bursting out simultaneously with, "We're going to Italy!"

"Wait, so let me get this straight," said Beau. You're going to Italy, and the gift you decided to give all of us, was a painting depicting that trip?"

Grandpa Anthony laughed out raucously and then said, "Helen, I don't think they understand what's happening."

"What is happening, exactly?" asked Aunt Christine in confusion.

"We're all going to Italy!" he exclaimed. "We're taking all of you on an all-expenses paid, two-week trip, to Italy next year!"

The entire room erupted into hysteria as the words seeped in that we were all going to Italy as a family. Beau and I actually hugged each other in excitement, which if I'm being completely honest was more than slightly disturbing, and everyone else was shouting out words of gratitude and praise to both Grandma Helen and Grandpa Anthony for their generous and magnanimous gift.

"Okay, settle down everyone," said Grandma Helen. "I want to explain to all of you our itinerary." She watched as everyone quieted down, and then continued, "Now, the plan is to be in Italy for a total of 15 nights, and as you've probably figured out by now, each one of your paintings represents an Italian city that we will be visiting. I enlisted Carol's help in painting all of these for you, so please be sure to let her know that I did actually acknowledge her involvement," she curled her lip in irritation, "even though I could have killed her the other night for almost ruining the surprise."

"Oh, that's why you were acting so strangely after opening your gift the other night," said mom.

"Yes, it was, however, being the brilliant actress that I am, I was able to smooth over her blundering mishap, and save the day as I so often do." She quickly changed the subject back to the topic of Italy, "Anyway, as I was saying, each of your paintings represents where it is we will be visiting in Italy. We will arrive in Milan and then take the train to head north to Varenna, where we will spend three glorious nights on Lake Como, as referenced by Christine's painting."

Grandpa Anthony then pointed over to mom and Beau's paintings of Tuscany and Pisa and said, "And then after Lake Como, we'll head south a bit, down to the Toscana region to see Florence, Pisa, and a few other medieval villages located in that area."

"And the wineries, darling!" added Grandma Helen. "Don't forget about all of the wineries we'll be visiting."

"How long will we be staying in Tuscany?" asked mom.

"Four nights, dear," she answered. "Plenty of time for you to enjoy the beautiful landscape you've coveted for so long."

"After Tuscany," said Grandpa Anthony, "We'll make our way down to Rome and spend two nights there, visiting all of the historical sites including the Colosseum, Palatine Hill, Spanish Steps, and the Roman Forum, just to name a few."

"And then we'll spend the last five nights of our trip in Positano, and tour around the Amalfi coast to see Capri, Sorento, and Ravello," smiled Grandma Helen.

"I'm honestly speechless," said mom. "I don't know what to say, or even how to thank you."

"Yes, thank you so much," said dad appreciatively. "This is literally a dream vacation for us, and the fact that we can all go together as a family means more than you'll ever know."

"Well, we've been wanting to do this for a long time," said Grandpa Anthony. "You and Olivia have done so much for us, letting us build a house on your property, that we wanted to do something nice and return the favor."

"So, when exactly are we going?" asked Aunt Christine.

"We decided on May, dear," answered Grandma Helen. "The theater doesn't have any productions going on at that time, so my schedule is completely free." She turned to dad, "I hope that will work for you, darling."

"I have plenty of vacation time saved up, so no need to worry about me," he winked.

"Oh, isn't this wonderful?" marveled Grandma Helen. "Two weeks in an Italian paradise, eating, drinking, and trying not to kill each other!"

CHAPTER TWENTY-FIVE

Christmas morning was finally here, and the heavenly scent of sausage balls wafted throughout the house, penetrating my dreams and awakening me from a deep slumber. After lying in bed a few minutes, I forced myself to get up so that I could help mom in the kitchen. Christmas morning tended to keep her incredibly busy, so I knew that she would appreciate my coming down to help her. As I descended the stairs, I was surprised to see how quiet and still the house was. Normally, there would be a flurry of activity and tons of noise, but when I came into the living room, I only found mom, quietly sitting in the bay window serenely sipping her coffee.

"Merry Christmas, mom," I said, coming up behind her.

"Merry Christmas, baby," she said, turning to face me.

"Dad was right, it did turn out to be a white Christmas after all," I said, taking a seat next to her. "Is everything okay?"

"Oh, yes, honey, everything's fine," she smiled. "I've just always found the snow to be so calming and peaceful, and I wanted to make sure I woke up early enough to spend a little time enjoying it before the chaos ensued." She looked longingly out the window, "It reminds me so much of a Thomas Kinkade painting, tranquil and calm, I just thought it prudent to get up and soak it all in before your brothers start trampling all over it, pelting each other with snowballs." She returned her attention back over to me, "So, how did you sleep?"

"I slept great," I yawned. "How about you?"

"Well, other than being awakened at one in the morning by your brother asking me for a sleeping pill, I slept relatively well," she said. "I swear, that child is almost thirteen years old; you would think that he'd be able to contain his excitement a little bit better. it's honestly like living with a four-year-old sometimes."

"You didn't give him one, did you?" I asked.

"Absolutely not," she shook her head vehemently. "Although I can't say I wasn't tempted."

The timer went off, alerting us that the first batch of sausage balls were ready, so I followed her amiably into the kitchen and watched as she donned a pair of oven mitts. "Addie, honey, would you mind placing some paper towels on that plate over there?" She pulled two trays out from the oven and immediately set them on the stovetop, "These things are delicious, but they have a tendency to be way too greasy."

"Oh, but it's the grease that makes them so good," smiled dad, joining us in the kitchen.

"Merry Christmas, honey," said mom.

"Merry Christmas, beautiful," he said, giving her a quick peck on the cheek. He wrapped me up in a giant hug, "Thanks for getting up and helping your mom with everything this morning, pumpkin."

"I really haven't done much, these were already in the oven when I came downstairs," I said.

"Yes, but she did mix them up yesterday and roll them into balls, so it made everything much easier on me this morning," smiled mom.

"Merry Christmas!" said Brian, happily taking a seat at the counter. "I hope everybody slept well."

"Merry Christmas," we answered simultaneously.

Aunt Christine shuffled in behind him, "Yeah, merry Christmas," she mumbled. "Please tell me there's coffee."

Mom silently handed her a cup three-quarters of the way full, set the cream and sugar down in front of her, and looked over at Brian, "We try not to say too much to her until she's had her morning coffee, she tends to be a bit surly and volatile, if we do."

"Yes, I learned that lesson the hard way a few months ago," he laughed. "I've since learned to curb my enthusiasm until she's had enough time to let the caffeine get into her system."

"You know I can still hear the two of you, right?" she muttered irritably.

"Hey, mom, are the sausage balls ready?" Ezra called out from the top of the stairs.

"Merry Christmas, to you too, Ezra," she shouted back.

He plodded downstairs, kissed mom on the cheek, and said, "Merry Christmas, are the sausage balls ready?"

She lifted the platter and he greedily popped one into his mouth, "Mmm, these things are so good, please tell me we have more."

"I just put another batch in the oven, so go ahead and help yourself to as many as you'd like," said mom. "Just be sure that you don't eat so much that you end up making yourself sick."

"I only did that once, when I was ten, mom," he rolled his eyes. "You've really got to let that go; you remind me of it every single holiday."

"Yes, well, you have a tendency to allow your eyes to be bigger than your stomach, Ezra, so I'm just being cautious," she lovingly patting his cheek.

We were well into the next batch of sausage balls and a second pot of coffee when Grandma Helen and Grandpa Anthony walked through the back door.

"Merry Christmas, my darlings!" trilled Grandma Helen.

"Merry Christmas, everyone," said Grandpa Anthony.

"Olivia, darling, are those the sausage thingies you always like to make?" she asked, pouring herself a cup of coffee. She peered over at the platter sitting on the counter and scrunched her nose, "Why are they all glistening like that, are they covered in grease?"

"They're made with sausage and cheese, mother, so yes, there's going to be some grease" answered mom. "But don't worry, Addie and I made sure to absorb as much as we could before plating them."

"Well, you can never be too careful," she said. "Southern cuisine is certainly not my area of expertise, but I do know that it's plagued with an overabundance of fat and grease, both of which are known to cause obesity, heart disease, and diabetes. At least with Italian food, you know you're getting fresher, natural ingredients, and only the healthiest of fats. You would do well to remember that, dear." She sipped her coffee, "So, are there any pastries?"

"Well, there's raspberry coffee cake and cinnamon rolls, if you'd rather have that," said mom. "Because, you know, processed sugar and cholesterol is so much better for you."

"Ooh, yes, that would be lovely, darling," she cooed. "Tell me, did you fry up any bacon?"

Aunt Christine could see Brian trying to make sense of the conversation taking place, so she leaned in close and said, "It's better to not ask any questions and just go along with the crazy, trust me."

"Presents!" yelled Beau, running down the stairs and into the kitchen.

Mom calmly stepped aside so that he could see the large platter of sausage balls sitting on the counter, "But first, sustenance!" He grabbed a few and placed them on a napkin, "You know, I really think we should start celebrating weekly with these things; I feel like we're limiting ourselves with only serving them on Thanksgiving, Christmas, and Easter."

"I'm pretty sure you'd tire of them, if we did," said mom.

"Nah, not possible," he said, shoving the last one in his mouth. "So, when can we open gifts?"

"I tell you what, why don't you go ahead and start separating everyone's gifts out into individual piles and then we'll all come in once that's done," said dad.

"That should buy us at least 15 minutes," muttered mom into her coffee.

"Oh, I already did that," he proclaimed proudly.

"What, when did you have time to do that?" asked mom.

"Last night when you so rudely refused to give me sleeping pill to help me fall asleep," he said grabbing another sausage ball. "I figured I'd just go ahead and use my suffering to be productive and efficient, since you know, it's Christmas, a time for giving."

"Well, that was certainly a smart way to make use of your time," said mom. "What's the likelihood of me seeing that same kind thinking when we start school back up in a few weeks?"

"Listen, you and I both know that you don't want to know the answer to that question, so I'm just going to politely act as if I didn't hear you." He then darted into the living room, "Okay, people, let's get this show on the road!"

***

Forty minutes later, we found ourselves sitting amongst a sea of opened gifts, emptied stockings, and trash bags filled to the brim with crumpled wrapping paper, card tags, and bows. Beau sat happily in his new gaming chair, carefully inspecting all of his newly acquired benefactions, while the rest of us spoke animatedly about our upcoming trip to Italy. Mom, Grandma Helen, and Aunt Christine were discussing all of the wineries they were planning on visiting, while dad, Grandpa Anthony, and Ezra discussed all of the historical sites and castles they were planning on touring. As I sat there listening, I looked up to see Brian standing alone in the kitchen, watching the conversations unfold with tremendous interest.

"They're just excited, I don't think they mean to leave you out," I said, walking up next to him.

"What's that?" he asked. "Oh, no, I'm not feeling left out, I'm just thinking about something, that's all."

"Is everything alright?" I asked.

"Yeah, everything's fine," he smiled assuredly. "Would you excuse me, Addie, there's something I really need to go and do." He took a deep breath and walked over to where Aunt Christine was sitting, sweetly taking her hand and gently pulling her to her feet. He cleared his throat and said, "Um, if all of you wouldn't mind indulging me for a moment, I'd like to take this opportunity to give Christine one more gift."

"I certainly hope it's nicer than that endless array of dowdy hiking gear you just gifted to her, dear," mumbled Grandma Helen.

"Mother, stop!" said Aunt Christine through gritted teeth.

Brian laughed good naturedly, "I believe you're going to approve of this one, Helen."

He slowly bent down on one knee, pulled out a beautiful marquis cut diamond ring, and held it out to her, "Christine, ever since the moment you walked into my life, I haven't stopped smiling. You are my best friend, my one constant, and I love you more than I ever thought I could love anybody. You are my home, my true north, and the very embodiment of what I always imagined love to be. I know that you have been hurt in the past, but if you will allow me to, I promise to spend the rest of my life making you as happy as you've made me. You are the air that I breathe and the one person I know I can't live without. Will you please do me the honor of marrying me and making me the happiest man alive?"

"Oh, my god, yes!" she exclaimed. "Yes, of course I'll marry you."

He slipped the ring onto her finger and she immediately embraced him, tears rolling down her face, "A thousand times, yes!"

"I love you so much," he whispered into her ear.

"Ahh, Chrissy, you're getting married!" shouted mom. She pushed Brian out of the way and grabbed Aunt Christine's hand, "Let me see the ring!"

"A wedding, oh, darling, that's wonderful!" exclaimed Grandma Helen. "We'll need to plan it around my theater schedule, but I believe I have some free time in September."

"Oh, my gosh, I can't believe you're getting married, I'm so excited for you!" I said, hugging her tightly.

"I think I'm still in shock," said Aunt Christine, "Look at me, I'm shaking."

"Yes, well, the excitement will eventually wear off, dear" dismissed Grandma Helen, with a wave of her hand. "Now, onto more important matters, like my outfit. Christine, darling, what do you think your colors are going to be, I need to make sure that I coordinate." She curled her lip, "Just please, nothing orange, dear, you know how much I despise anything that falls under that particular color scheme. Oh, and nothing in yellow either, it always makes me look so washed out; I will say, I do look fabulous in teal, so that may honestly be the best option, or black, I've always looked extraordinarily elegant in black."

"Yes, I'll try to keep all of that in mind, mother," she said, rolling her eyes.

"So, I guess this makes you my new uncle," said Beau sidling up next to Brian. He shook his head dolefully and snickered, "You have absolutely no idea what you've just hitched your wagon to, do you?" He strutted back over to his stockpile of gifts, "Oh man, this is going to be fun to watch."

"Congratulations, Brian, we're happy to have you join the family," said Ezra patting him on the back.

"Welcome to the family, son," said Grandpa Anthony shaking his hand. "I'd say everything went pretty much according to plan, wouldn't you?"

"Wait, you knew about this, dad?" asked Aunt Christine.

"And you didn't think it important enough to tell me?" asked Grandma Helen, her voice going up an octave. "How could you not tell me something like this, Anthony?"

"Because I asked him not to," answered Brian, "I wasn't entirely sure when I was going to ask Christine to marry me, but I knew I wanted Anthony's blessing before I did, so rather than risk anyone accidentally letting something slip, I figured the best thing to do was just keep it between the two of us for a while."

"How long is awhile?" asked Grandma Helen, slightly perturbed.

"It was only a few weeks, honey," soothed Grandpa Anthony. "You were busy planning the Angel Tree celebration, anyway."

"Oh, my gosh, honey, that's so sweet of you," gushed Aunt Christine. "I can't believe you asked my father for my hand in marriage."

"Well, it was the right thing to do," said Brian. "Your father was incredibly kind and supportive, and I really appreciated him taking the time to help me figure everything out." He pointed to her hand "He even helped me pick out that ring, which is why it's a marquis, he said it was your favorite cut of diamond."

"Oh, my gosh, dad, thank you so much," wept Aunt Christine, warmly embracing him. "I can't tell you how much that means to me."

"Well, I, for one, can honestly say that we are beyond thrilled to have you join our family, darling," cooed Grandma Helen. "You may find us a bit outlandish and excessive at times, but I have a feeling you're going to fit right in."

"Us?" asked mom, raising her brow skeptically. "No, you're the outlandish one, mother."

"Oh, Christine, darling, I simply cannot wait to start planning this wedding!" exclaimed Grandma Helen. She draped her arm around her, pulling her in tight, "You know, dear, if you play your cards right, I may just be willing to pull double duty as both mother of the bride and the entertainment; in fact, we can just go ahead and hire Colin to come and do the music since he already carries my set list and knows exactly how I do everything."

"Colin does Karaoke at Sullivan's, mother, he's not a DJ," said Aunt Christine. She then looked imploringly over at mom and mouthed the words, "Help me."

While Aunt Christine and Grandma Helen continued deliberating over details of a wedding that wasn't even on anyone's radar up until five minutes ago, dad leaned in close to Brian and said quietly, "You just jumped headfirst into the cuckoo's nest, my friend, I hope you brought your straight jacket."

"Okay, everyone, listen" interjected mom. "We're going to have plenty of time to hash all of this out later, so rather than getting caught up in all the minutiae, why don't we slow things down a bit and just focus our attention on the celebration of Christmas, and Brian and Christine's engagement."

"Does that mean it's mimosa time, darling?" grinned Grandma Helen. "I do so love a good celebratory mimosa!"

"Sure, why not?" smiled mom. "Chrissy, would you mind grabbing the champagne from the outside refrigerator while I get the glasses set up?"

"Yeah, I can do that," she said.

"Oh, and girls," said Grandma Helen with a gleam in her eye, "Please be sure to Hellenize mine!"

The End.

A LETTER FROM TIFFANY

Thank you so much for reading *Jingled and Jangled: A Delightfully Dysfunctional Familial Christmas,* the second installment in the Delightfully Dysfunctional series. I hope you had as much fun reading it as I had writing it, and if you haven't already, please be sure to check out the first book in the series, *Crazed and Confused: A Delightfully Dysfunctional Familial Memoir.* As I'm sure you're well aware, the Jenkins are near and dear to my heart, so you can rest assured that I have quite a few more books planned for the series, with the third installment heading your way by late 2024.

I love hearing from my readers, so please, always feel free to drop me a message anytime via Facebook, Instagram, and/or my personal website. Interaction with you is what motivates me to write, so please, always feel free to reach out and let me know your thoughts. Facebook and Instagram are also where I plan to be sharing information on new and upcoming books, major announcements, book signings, etc., so please make sure to follow me there so that you can stay informed.

Facebook Page: https://www.facebook.com/TiffanyRyanAuthor

Instagram Page: https://www.instagram.com/tiffany_ryan_author

Website: tiffanyryanwrites.com

Sincerely,

Tiffany

ACKNOWLEDGMENTS

It takes a village to raise a child, and a group of talented and selfless individuals to help an Indy author publish a book. I have been unbelievably blessed by the people God has chosen to place in my path, and for that, I will be eternally grateful.

Having said that, I would like to thank Mandy Oliver and Raven Lynn Spalding for lending their time and talents in helping me bring the Jenkins to life. Thank you for always motivating me with your kind words and your gentle corrections. Raven, you always catch my mistakes and missing quotation marks, so on behalf of my readers, thank you. Mandy, your friendship means the world to me, and the fact that you selflessly and willingly give not only your time, but also your talent, in creating graphics to help spread the word about my books, means more to me than you will ever know.

I would also like to thank my mother, Kathi Catalano, for being my loudest cheerleader, and for talking incessantly to anyone that will listen about her daughter that likes to write funny stories.

Gabriel and McKenna, you will always be my greatest accomplishment in life, and I love you more than you will ever know.

Lastly, I would like to thank my husband, Blake, for always supporting me and encouraging me to spread my wings and fly. You've always had faith in me, even when I didn't have faith in myself, and for that, I will always love you.

www.ingramcontent.com/pod-product-compliance
Lightning Source LLC
Chambersburg PA
CBHW051512260626
47162CB00008B/2929